Jojoba Essence

By

Najen Mack

Jojoba Essence © 2013 by Najen Mack

This book is a work of fiction. Any references to historical events, real people, or real locales are used fictitiously. Any names, characters, places and incidents are the product of the imagination, and any resemblance to the actual events or locales or persons, living or dead, is entirely coincidental.

All rights are reserved. No part of this book may be reproduced in any manner whatsoever, including Internet usage, without written permission from the publisher, except by review.

Printed in the United States of America

ISBN: 978-0-9837771-6-8

Cover Design: Moe Scriber, Modern Day Hippie
Editing/Typesetting: Carla M. Dean, U Can Mark My Word

Sales inquiries should be forwarded to:

(Najen.LLC and Vantage Point)
(Duluth, Minnesota 55806)

Acknowledgements

At the beginning of this journey I started this to heal myself. I was foolish enough to believe that this book was about me. I needed an outlet. I needed a platform to express feelings ignored, to my surprise I reached out and met many women who in turn thought that their voice had been found through these pages. I want to thank God for His unwavering hand in making the connections over the years with these beautiful women possible. I want to thank God for his grace, patients and unconditional love.

I would like to thank the original Najen.LLC team Jacque, Bonnie and Brent; you all listen to my stories, ideas and helped with the first editing process. You all were so patient with me. So I thank you and will never forget what you all did, page after page. I love you.

To my children your patience for allowing me quiet time, and staying at the daycare when I spent hours in the studio, this is for us. To Tatiana KEEP PUSHING FORWARD. If only a legacy is found; it is all worth it. I Love each of you. To my sisters who knew this was possible and thought out loud "hurry up and get done we want to hear the whole thing instead of a page at a time", Lucretia "the diva" Jones and

Sade "I'm going shopping" Sandidge. To the 5am three way phone calls. They will never understand why we laugh so hard, through it all". To my mother and father the talent came from somewhere. I would like to thank my mother for the educating me on the secret of life, motivation, determination, faith of a mustard seed and love of the Almighty. Thanks Joe Carter for being you and the continued support. To Mrs. Shawn Coleman your conversations have taken me over the hardest moments in my life, thank you darling. To Bobbi Jo Potter thank you for reminding me that my leadership has created even more leaders, Loves!

There has been one friend, gentle heart and love who worked with me to open many closed doors, thank you Orsen Mcgee of Baltimore, MD. You couldn't have come into my life at a better time.

To my Willie Mae McEntyre you were great, you pushed me and accepted me for the woman I was, and the woman that I was to become. You called me weekly just to ensure I was still working on goals. I love you and even though you may not see this manuscript in print I carry you with me daily in spirit and actions. Never to be forgotten. Last but not least, to Cindy Henry of Duluth, Minnesota, your understanding is worth so much more than the payments you received, thank you.

I want to thank Mo of Modern Day Hippie www.moderndayhipie.co for your hard work and dedication to this project.

If I have forgotten you please write your name in this space _____, and what I should be thanking you for.

Sincerely,

Najen

Jojoba Essence

Chapter 1
The Revenge

Touch me. Hold me.

The words played over in her head like a broken record. Sitting in the corner, she could hear, but she couldn't see. Her thoughts just continued playing that same song. This couldn't be real. Looking back to November 17, 2008, she didn't see her life there. *That coward!* All these years she stuck through the good, the bad, the ups and the downs. And for what? So it could turn out like this? He actually expected to receive understanding from her after torching her, lighting her soul on fire.

Yes, I know I made a few mistakes. Hell, a lot of mistakes. But, I was honest about my mistakes. I regretted everything I did. I repented. Still, day in and day out, he has constantly thrown the things I've done in my face. He has to be kidding me with this, though. He didn't even have the gall to tell me. No, I had to walk in on them cradled in the shower, making love on my marble floor. Bubbles were all over the walls, candles burning, and Gerald Levert in the background singing about needing love. He needs love? Seems to me like he had all the love he needed. With me, he always had it his way. Now, it will be my turn to have it my way.

With her holding that knife to his throat, it seemed he couldn't get a word out.

He, the head of my household who was once too strong to crawl, is now too weak to stand tall through it all. This man is a joke.

No more moans. Mumbling, crying, and whining were all she heard. He must have thought she wouldn't flip. Probably thought she would smile and join in.

"Baby, let me soap you up," she had heard him say.

She looked and listened for over an hour. She couldn't breathe. She exhaled and inhaled like a spy on a World War III mission. She was the Russian spy, and her country was depending on her to break the code of "What the fuck is going on?" Lives would truly not be the same when she made it home with this information.

Tears ran down her face when she discovered her husband loved another soul. Watching him caress this chocolate body as they washed each other's hair with her favorite Shea Butter shampoo sent rage through her.

"Baby, I love how that smells on you," were his next words.

As she listened to him express how he genuinely loved this soul, she almost regurgitated the breakfast he had cooked for her that morning.

"Are you sure this is okay?" the person asked.

"She doesn't care," he replied. "She knows about us."

Mary Jane damn near died. She damn near swallowed her tongue when she heard the lie flow so easily from his mouth, every word cutting her deeply and slowly! If blood flowed upward, her soul would have burst. This man was a true heartbreaker. She needed to know; she needed to see how he reacted to another. She wanted to see would he do the same things to them as he had done to her just a few short hours ago. Would he fall to his knees and take them in his mouth? Would he take his lingam and put it headfirst into their mouth? What would be the first move?

So, she watched. Regretfully, she watched. She watched and hated herself for doing so. She was mad. Still, she watched as they kissed. Not just a casual kiss, but a passionate, make-love-to-me kiss. Down the shoulders, across the elbows, and licking each fingertip, they enjoyed her husband. This person was in love with her husband. They were making love to her husband in ways she had yet to discover his body. Why not allow her to do that?

His lingam hung long against the shower wall. His shadow allowed his manhood to be a foot long. It was thick, its veins bulging out. He held the shower wall as if he was ready to climb it. If not for the water flowing off the wall, she believed he would have been a spider dangling off its web, a web of deceit or cum, whichever would have been thick enough to hold him.

She watched this love machine spread her husband's ass cheeks and insert a finger into his rectum. He enjoyed it. They touched. They touched some more. The "other" person rubbed him, kissing him down his back in the process. They told him to relax, just as her husband had asked her to do that morning. Her husband called out their name, which sounded so familiar to Mary Jane.

The more she heard, the more rage seeped out of her. She blacked out. When she came to, she was soaking wet and standing over them. She had jumped in the shower with them. In the process, the candles were knocked over; the fire was out. However, the burning inside of her remained. The devil had complete control of her exhausted, idle hand. The blade dug into her hand. She closed her eyes. She wanted blood, but did not want to see it. The mysterious person had disappeared. Where did they go? She wasn't sure, but her I-love-the-finger-in-my-booty husband was trapped and speechless.

When she thought back to her affair, she viewed their situation as being something beautiful. It didn't start out as an affair right away. They were friends, but got caught up looking for what they should have gotten at home. They were unsure of what they were doing. Confused! They were sexy, though. A hug, a small kiss, an "I love you" spoken when one of them needed to hear it. They never violated either of their homes. On the other hand, Mary Jane's husband wanted to get caught. He was a criminal looking for forgiveness, but that was unforgivable.

One night, her husband decided not to go home. He just didn't show up after a meeting. She cried and cried until she was unable to shed any more tears. She called the hospitals, jails, friends, families, and local bars, but no one had heard from him or seen him. Mary Jane went to his job. The doors were locked. No signs of trouble. No glass broken. His car was gone. She was bluffed. She went home and placed a call. She called a hotel, made reservations, and then called her friend Star to comfort her.

"Can you come?" she asked. "I have a few dollars. We can go to the casino downstairs. I don't want to talk. I don't want to think. Can you simply come?"

A few long hours and half a bottle of Grey Goose later, Mary Jane was fine. She wasn't crying anymore. They were in the casino having such an exuberant time that she forgot the reason why they were there. But, just as she felt herself going numb, it hit her again. She was reminded that her dear husband, Cole, was missing in action. Mary Jane almost hoped something was wrong just so she could feel guilty. Somehow, though, she knew he was straight.

After letting loose some more, they decided to go back upstairs to the room. She dashed for the bed. Her friend was as drunk as her, but they didn't care. Star came clean, telling Mary Jane that her husband didn't come home either. That's why it was not such a big deal that she came to the hotel.

"Those bitches!" they said aloud in unison, then laughed.

Hungry, they ordered room service. By the time the food came, they were profoundly kissing, their tongues wrestling. Mary Jane was sweet, a fresh scent. Star took one of her breasts and sucked her nipple slowly. The way she handled her let Mary Jane know she was out to please the both of them, not just for her own personal pleasure. As Star sucked, Mary Jane moaned. She was lost in the moment. Mary Jane skimmed inside of her. She was nervous. She didn't know how far to go.

Star had this way of erotically looking up at Mary Jane while massaging her skin with the flesh of her lips. Mary Jane didn't want this woman to stop. She wanted her to continue down her legs to her womanhood. She wanted Star to be her husband, to relish what she had to offer.

Star called Mary Jane with her eyes. Turning so she was now underneath Star with her face between Star's thighs, Mary Jane started moving her hips to the beat inside her head, feeding Star a mouthful full of pussy. While serving herself to Star, she moved Star's satin panties to the side. It was sexy. She closed her eyes and loved her, all of her. The feeling she experienced was magical. Star smelled so wonderful.

With each passing moment, Star became wetter as the two dined on each other. When Mary Jane smacked her ass, Star lost control and called out, "Mary-Jane!"

Mary Jane was taming her, pleasing her. Star became so caught up in being pleased that she forgot about doing her part. She stopped physically pleasing Mary Jane. So, Mary Jane grabbed a hand full of Star's sandy blonde hair and forced her face back in her pussy. Mary Jane wanted her to find sanity in her womanhood. She smacked her backside again; it bounced. Not long after, Star came all over her face. It was their first time, and Mary Jane was able to make Star climax.

Wanting Mary Jane to experience the same pleasure, Star rolled over, and while lying breathless on her back, she pulled Mary Jane on top of her. She didn't position Mary Jane's roundness on her face, though. She lowered her on the strap-on she was now donning and fucked Mary Jane with her manhood. She fucked her as if this had been her plan. She fucked her harder than any man ever had. This was sexually more than Mary Jane could handle, and before long, she exploded in ecstasy.

Since Star's erection was made of rubber and not flesh, she kept going. With each movement, Star did something different. She would pull Mary Jane's hair. Then she would grab her throat. Just when Mary Jane thought she was about to pass out, Star released her hold and flipped her over on her stomach to deliver some doggy style treatment. Star had her tongue, fingers, and a fake-flesh lingam all in Mary Jane's yoni at one time. An assassination of lovemaking was taking place and Mary Jane didn't mind. Really, she was not concerned.

This was one night. Afterwards, Mary Jane would go home and not be mad. This was her great revenge.

She woke up comfortable in the arms of the same sex. Star woke up first and kissed Mary Jane awake.

"We were not wrong," she told her.

She said it as if she knew what Mary Jane was thinking. Maybe Mary Jane should have been thinking that, but she wasn't. She was more concerned with the smell of her breath. Mary Jane smiled as Star held her.

Star looked Mary Jane in the eyes and said, "If just for one night, I had you and treated you like the woman you should always be treated like when your body is being touched. If only for one night, you were mine."

Those were the last words spoken before they left the room. Star walked to her car, and Mary Jane walked in the opposite direction. Even though Mary Jane showered, she could still smell Star on her flesh. She could smell the strawberries of the shampoo and conditioner. That incident involving her husband was far from that, though. That was not sexy. That was sick and perverted.

Her husband was getting sexually excited by a strong, tattooed man…a man who looked like he had just gotten out of prison. He hid in the closet; he was a bitch for sure. A mad black woman, Mary Jane knew who wouldn't run. Mary Jane saw the blood she wanted to see. It was her blood from holding the knife too tightly. Then it was her weak-minded, finger-in-the-butt-loving husband. He bled like a fresh catfish. She loved every moment of it until she realized what she had done. Mary Jane had cut his fingers off, all four of them that had run across the flesh of another soul. After that, she blacked out. It was well over the amount of blood she wanted to see.

When she came to, Mary Jane found herself handcuffed to a hospital bed. He didn't press charges. This embosom of love he tried to give her was a day too late. The state picked up the case and pressed charges instead. As a result, she was doing three and a half years and now a felon.

Chapter 2
Life Changes

Every day Mary Jane was there she wanted to break a window and escape. The orange jumpsuit clashed with the grey walls. She loathed the person who designed that place and the clothing they wore. Brick by brick, she wanted out of that cell. She had fallen into a trap of Hell. Looking up at the lamp that she so often wanted to smash, she thought of how it was too damn bright. She hated when five o'clock in the morning came. First, she heard the siren and then the clicking of the bars. Before she knew it, the bright light came on and the bars slid open. Next, the correctional officers sung off the same numbers as they did every day. Then they would get to her: #096734.

Mary Jane had not been referred to by her name in three years, only a number. She had been reduced from the woman she should have been to a six-digit number that would have no meaning if she did not exist in that caged Hell that housed individuals who had anger issues…those who screamed and smeared excrement on their walls in hopes of pissing off the correctional officers who laughed insanely at them. They reported to work to watch and enjoy the daily antics of the circus clowns.

They appeared to be animals in a zoo of selfish fools. Their crimes overshadowed who they were as people. Violence, cries, tears, and fears. Friendships lost, loved ones forgotten. Mary Jane once wore double-breasted coats with button-down shirts, matching it with single-split skirts and French heels. She wore name-brand clothing to cover her lavish lavender-smelling skin. She had purchased the best of everything from food to perfume. She was the best.

However, now she was nothing more than a kitchen aid, an individual who prepared meals for hundreds of inmates. She just wanted to do her time and get out of there. Having money only made her a target for trouble. The women learned through the grapevine that she was imprisoned because she had cut her husband's fingers off after catching him with his male lover. Instead of walking away, she needed to feel his blood; she wanted to see his tears as they rolled down his face. She needed an explanation. Instead, what she got was prison time!

It took a long time to think about what she had done, what she could do differently, and what she would do when she got home. One day, she would go home. She would lie on her bed and be thankful to God for peacefulness. She would wash her hair, using a new shampoo with a scent she had yet to smell. She will order food in and laugh at the madness that landed her in such a place. She would no longer have to eat the prison's insipid food. She would enjoy sushi and soul food. Her first cocktail of choice would be a Yellow Bird, and sipping it would only be the beginning of living a lifestyle of freedom.

She wanted to stare into the eyes of the women of her favorite painting, The Fernand Léger by Le Petit Dejeuner. The women in that painting are full-figured with round hips, long black hair, and large breasts. When thinking about that painting, she wanted to cry, remembering a time when men appreciated women for their natural beauty. She had plans of owning Le Petit Dejeuner's entire collection. She wanted The Construction Workers, The Builders, and Still Life with a Beer Mug. They were realistic to our lives today. On the wall across from it hung the painting of Mother Courage II by Charles White, a self-taught man. They painted in Modern Era. These men were great during their time, and instead of her having a man of that nature, she had a man who wanted a man.

Mary Jane's last few months were the hardest of her bid. She received a letter from her best friend. Unsure what to think when she received it, her only fear was that her friend would desert her, leaving Mary Jane alone in the horrible state she was in. The two often laughed through their letters and cried over the phone. After receiving the letter, Mary Jane waited until she was back in her 4x4 home before reading it. She wanted privacy. She needed not to share her friend or her friend's words. Mary Jane wanted her to herself, no interruptions.

Later that evening, once she was no longer worried about the heaviness of the letter or anyone peeking over her shoulder, she read aloud the words that flowed too easily yet so heavily.

My Dearest Mary Jane,

Life has brought us together, and without a flash of light, we are there for each other. I remember as children we would laugh at the smallest things and cry at nothing. Not bullies and far from pushovers. Our parents didn't understand our love. They assumed we were selfish because we did not allow anyone in our circle. At school, we were weird. Holding hands and ignoring the rest of our fellow classmates made us stick out the most.

My earliest memory of us is our first day of school in first grade, and both of our parents kissing us goodbye before rushing off to work. It tickles me when I think back to how stubborn we were. They cried, and we wiped their tears while explaining how their upbringing had brought us far enough. Therefore, it was time to let go so we could grow up to be great women. As they walked away, we turned to each other, and within seconds, we were a team. The other kids cried and we laughed. Whenever one of us became scared, it was our internal souls that grew, becoming one! We could feel each other's pain. We would hold hands and comfort each other before any teacher ever knew we were in distress.

Over the years, our love grew stronger and continued through our college years. You changed majors, and it drove me crazy. You were lost in time, but I couldn't help. Your sureness of life made me love you more. We have loved each other through bad marriages. Most importantly, when you found me passed out and covered in blood in my own house after being raped, you carried me and protected me. That internal love…how I love that bond. Just as our love has grown, our internal souls have grown, also.

This will not come to me as a surprise if you know something is wrong. Unlike you, when trouble comes, my vocal cords will not allow such trouble to be vocalized. I have always written trouble on paper and allowed my deepest thoughts to flow. Please do not ask why I didn't call sooner. We are old enough to know why I didn't call. The fear I did not have as a child has settled in over the years and you have become my voice.

"Stella, what is wrong? Why are you dragging up old memories that we have not spoken about in years?" you ask. Well, the short version to this story is, I went in for my yearly pap and my cancerous cervical cells have returned. Returned? I know you're wondering what I'm talking about. Well, when we were sixteen and I went to the doctor, I became distant and you couldn't understand why. You begged me to tell you because you could feel something was wrong. You thought I had sex and did not share the intimate details. Then you thought my standoffish behavior was because my dad appeared out of nowhere. I smile while thinking about how for weeks you wouldn't let it go. You were right to feel that emptiness in the pit of your stomach. That was exactly how I felt.

It was in the first stage, referred to as dysplasia. They did a loop, which is a form of surgery. I was awake during the procedure, but it was not that painful. They found the abnormal cells in several different places. My options were easy at the time because they caught it at an early stage. I chose the cone biopsy. During this procedure, they removed my abnormal cells by loop electrode excision (using wire loops heated by electric current). Because cervical cancer appears slowly in the body, it is possible to stop it and control it, if a woman gets her yearly Pap smear. This reason alone is why I ask you all the time to go to the doctor. I love you enough to pressure you to love yourself. You hate doctors and I hate pain, but they are two things we cannot live without.

Once they removed the cells, I had to wait two weeks for my results. When I received them, I wanted to run to you. I wanted to share with you the fear I held in my heart, my soul, but the truth is I didn't want you to see me so weak. I made the decision to live life to the best of my ability. I was positive for cancer, and there was nothing I could do but wait to see what my next option was.

I had tons of questions. What treatments are available? What was my life expectancy? How much pain will I experience? The treatments would depend on the stage of the cancer, the size of the tumor, my age, and my desire to have children. He gave me many options, one of which I must admit scared me because of my shallowness of being bald. I am now in the stages of invasive cervical cancer, and there are few options available to me. Surgery, radiation, and chemotherapy were my options. The treatment for this form of *cancer is radical hysterectomy, which is the removal of my uterus, fallopian tubes, ovaries, adjacent lymph nodes, and part of the vagina. When my doctor explained this to me, I looked at him as if he was nuts. He wanted my womanhood. What was I to live for besides my cats? I was confused about life and questioned my worth on earth. Had I been such a terrible person that I deserved such a thing? I was angry and hurt, yet thankful for the life I did have. Worst of all, if I did not make a decision soon, there would be no decision to make at all. Death was near and I would not allow it to take me without a fight. So, I made the choice to have the surgery. I didn't go bald, but I lost weight.*

Unfortunately, my worse fear came true. When they began the surgery, they noticed the cancer had spread throughout my body, and there was nothing else they could do other than make me comfortable for the time being.

If you are reading this, I have passed without explaining the love I carry for you. Please don't be upset or angry. The joy of having you in my life was more than any true friend could ask for, and at this time, I only ask this one thing of you. Please educate those near and far about this disease. Cervical cancer is a disease with little to no symptoms. There can be pelvic pain, discharge from your vagina, bleeding, and pain during sexual intercourse. Though these symptoms can come from different issues, it is very important to get regular checkups. Hell, get extra checkups, if necessary. There are many factors to cervical cancer, but women with HPV (Human Papillomavirus) have an increased risk of getting it. Other risk factors are women who smoke cigarettes, give birth to many children, have many sexual partners, have a weak immune system, and believe it or not, use the pill (oral contraceptive) for birth control. At this time, there are no cures, but prevention is at an all-time high. As the medical field continues to learn more about this disease, they continue to believe the best prevention is safe sex and regular checkups.

As women, we need to learn not to fear our bodies or the important information we can gain from going to the doctors and asking questions. I ask you to share this information. I know you are angry with me, but do as I did with my students—educate women, both young and old. With that, I will leave you with this:

Friends
Women love their children; I had none.
Women cherish their husband; I left mine.
Women wear the true hat of the world; my hat would not be as colorful without you.
Women gain and lose friends all the time; losing you as my best friend, my only true friend is the hardest part of saying goodbye. Yet, I love you and pray daily that you will forgive my selfishness for not allowing you to endure a long drawn-out goodbye that you feel you need. No, I may not be here in the physical sense, but my presence will always be in your heart. Loving you was a choice given by God. For that, my passing is a peaceful one.

Loving you truly, Stella

Mary Jane could have stopped breathing and collapsed on the floor where she stood. "This has to be some kind of sick joke," she thought out loud, while pacing back and forth. She wanted…no, she needed to walk. Whom would she share this mercy with? Stella was her best friend…her only friend…who had stolen her goodbye because of selfishness. Stella did not care that Mary Jane was left alone. She did not fight long enough to see her come home. She gave up, thinking only about herself. Mary Jane believed she should have been there; she needed Stella to know she loved her. The tears fell as doubt began to show through her strength. Stella would not welcome her at the gate of freedom once she was released. Maybe things would not be the same when she got home. After all, Mary Jane had no one. Where would she turn?

Although there were more letters to open, she refused, afraid there may be more bad news. Throwing the rest of the mail in the corner, she climbed onto her bunk bed and didn't move for hours. Since Stella wasn't family, Mary Jane had to face the sad reality that she would not be allowed to go to the funeral.

Her body was dehydrated. She could not form a tear. Her mouth felt dry, and she wanted to pee, but nothing escaped from her. She was out of her natural state. Her skin was drier than normal, her face was pale, and her knees were weak. She was officially alone. She was thirty years old, and her deepest fear had come true. Rage exerted her worn flesh; her anger was a maelstrom in the pit of her soul. She had driven herself past madness with no arrow for control. She needed to see the psychiatrist, who would surely diagnose her as having PTSD, post-traumatic stress disorder. Whatever she was suffering from was killing her surface first and her soul last. Her soul looked into her eyes and laughed at the aging of her body. Her soul did not notice its home. She appeared young and full of life, while her flesh looked haggard.

Her friend had died, and the burden was too heavy for her to carry. Sweating profusely, she could have drowned in her sweat. Hearing fellow inmates yelling from afar, she drifted further from her present state. She wanted to be with her dear friend. She wanted her to know she had not only left behind family, but she had left her to deal with life alone. She felt selfish, ignorant to the actuality that she was not in her world. She was a friend who Mary Jane depended on. They were supposed to grow old together.

Awakening was harder than her fall to the floor. She had a splitting headache. Waking this time, she had bandages on her head and an IV in her hand. As a precaution, they had handcuffed her to the bed. She didn't want to hurt herself, but she surely wanted to die. She wanted her heart to stop beating against her chest. With each beat, she wanted to reach into her chest and pull her heart out from her rib cage. She had been forbidden at having true love and now robbed of a lifetime friend.

The heavy dose of morphine administered caused her to drift off to sleep. She really did not remember much at the time, only that she wanted to sleep. And that's what she did. As she watched the morphine drip into her arm, her thoughts found peace with her friend Stella by her side. They sat near the sea, allowing its breeze to cool them as they had their picnic. They dined on a simple hot pastrami croissant sandwich and wedges of fried bananas. Stella began the conversation talking about her day. Then, with the first bite of her sandwich, she smiled at Mary Jane and requested she let her go. With the second bite, she told her to stop holding on to the dirtiness of her husband's sexual deeds. She stated his deed was no dirtier than Mary

Jane's, that the beauty Mary Jane held on to regarding her own wrong sexual deed was not as beautiful as she wanted it to seem.

Although Stella could be harsh at times, her honesty is what made Mary Jane love her the most. She said what was on her mind and was frank about it. She hated that Mary Jane had a one-night stand with a woman. She didn't judge, but she didn't approve nor agree. She wanted to know what Mary Jane's husband had done to make her want to devour on the sex of another woman. She told Mary Jane that she had no business riding the flesh of a woman. The sweet scent of the woman's nectar across her lips was not a challenge that needed to be fulfilled. Mary Jane could not find the words to explain her actions. She was guilt ridden, and her embarrassment was more than she could handle.

Stella cradled Mary Jane's face with her right hand and waved with her left. Their picnic was over and they had to say goodbye. Before leaving, Stella left Mary Jane with these last words that would haunt her: *Life's challenges are not behind you; they are ahead of you.*

Chapter 3
Awakening Moments

After lying in the hospital bed for three days, Mary Jane's headache was finally gone and the IV had been removed. Now one hour from being back in her 4x4 cell, she wanted out of the infirmary more than she wanted out of prison. Having to get twenty-seven stitches in her head was the result of the blackout. Her inner being was free, but her body gave way to the shock and stress over losing her best friend.

Returning to her chambers was nothing short of what she expected. Apparently, there had been a fight on the yard earlier that the day. So, all the inmates were on lockdown. She never understood why women fight so much. They fight over hair, clothes, children, pride, and most of all, respect. They want their respect as much as men want theirs. Their pressure in the joint is the same as the pressure men experience on the streets. Being behind bars, they had to earn and keep their respect, just like anyone on the outside.

Back home in her cell, the removal of the handcuffs was a pleasure. Looking around, she found her home in disarray. She began remembering the emotions she felt. She looked in the mirror and recalled her skin being chalky. Her throat was desiccated, dry to the bone. She remembered gasping for air, wanting the tears that flowed down her cheeks to quench her thirst. Rain fell in the desert more often than fire flooded the sea. Yet, she was unable to breathe…her breath lost within the pipes of her body. She remembered the voices far off in the distance, the clicking of bars as they opened. She remembered the dream and Stella saying goodbye.

Once more, she looked at the mess she had left behind, the remaining mail she did not open and her unmade bed. Her personal hygiene products were thrown throughout the small space. Cleaning would be a breeze, though.

Letter by letter, she opened the envelopes. She received a letter from a forgotten friend who wanted to know how she was doing. It was unexpected...actually unwanted. The letter was from her Shea Butter beauty, which she hadn't heard from nor spoke with since her first court appearance. Emotionless to the words that flowed on the pages she held in her hand, she crumbled all eight of them. Words formed into letters to distract the natural course of her life. The words were meaningless. The small, charcoal-black ink spots on the paper let her know she had taken a break from writing to think of what she wanted to say. She was unsure of herself, and she was certain this was not something she yearned for.

Mary Jane received a letter from the DOC and one from her lawyer. She was not willing to fancy the idea of being freed. She wanted to sleep. So, she slipped the addressed envelopes under her flattened pillow and slept to the best of her ability.

Chapter 4
Mary Jane

Five o'clock a.m. First, the siren was heard and then the clicking of the bars. Before Mary Jane knew it, the bright light came on and the bars slid open. Numbers and more numbers were called out. Then they got to her: #096734. Every day she had the same beginning and the same ending. Today would begin differently, though.

The light would not bother her. She was prepared. She had awakened before the light came on. She was already washed and dressed. It was Thursday, laundry day. Pulling off the pillowcase, her letters fell to the floor. Eluding these letters was not an option. She was compelled to read them out of responsibility. A few months away from being free, unexpected letters was not something she looked forward to receiving.

While looking through her mail, more letters appeared. After reading her first letter from Stella, she was reluctant to open any more. This letter carried the scent of a male. It was strong. The smell was distinguishable. She knew that smell from a different life, a life she left behind only a few short years ago. This man was an interesting creature and had his way of getting everything he desired. There was a time he desired fortune and fame, which he retained six years after high school. He desired to have Mary Jane spread across a summer blanket on a white sandy beach. He accomplished that and even had someone videotape them. There was nothing he desired that he did not acquire. Now he was writing her for what? To gloat? To share his ideas of a new business that would keep him in the Fortune 500?

Holding the letter in her hand, she placed it close to her face and devoured his scent with her thoughts. She picked him apart with memories: his dark silver and emerald eyes; the black curls that hung over his ears; how his ears were stretchable; how his nose flared when he didn't understand something. Remembering these things would seem odd if she did not think of him daily.

She could recall the strength of his legs from running five miles every day. His bedroom facing the ocean, he would awaken to the left of his bed. Before opening his eyes, he would push a button on the remote that opened the vertical wooden blinds. Soothing jazz would start playing through the surround sound speakers above his bed. The small Bose speakers produced enough bass to push him out of bed. Before going to the bathroom to brush his teeth or wash his face, he would bend and pull his shoes from underneath the bed. While doing so, he remembered to thank God for his ability to bend down, but never did he thank God for the material things. The first time Mary Jane noticed him doing this, she asked why he only gave thanks for his ability to bend. His response was, "I could thank Him for an entire collection of things that He has allowed me to have as a result of my hard work, but all that could be taken away. Then what would I thank Him for? So, I figure why not thank Him for the things that matter the most, which are often the little things that most people take for granted. Be blessed for what man may try to take from you when you have nothing left, which is your peace of mind."

King is what she called him. His belief in God left her speechless. His faith was strong enough for the both of them. He was the one she lost due to not having patience. She wanted him to react to her in a certain way. She wanted him to worship her, but he refused. He worshiped one being and that being was God. Now she was looking at a letter from him and embracing the fact that he had thought of her. Saving this letter would be different from saving other letters.

Mary Jane opened it with ease. Taking the tip of a pencil, she used it as if it were an envelope opener. Being optimistic, she wanted to wait, but her nerves couldn't take it.

Dear Beautiful One,

This morning, I awakened wanting to taste you. I wanted to touch the smoothness of your breasts and lick the sweet juices of your bold, brown lips. I wanted to kiss the salt off your shoulders, while rubbing the hairs on your stomach and caressing my morning stiffness against the small of your back. Awakening to your scent has often crossed my mind.

This morning, I yearned to have you in my mouth, your legs wrapped around my neck, choking the last breath from my lungs as you release your wetness on the tip of my lips. As moisture began to fill my mouth, I swallowed it all, not missing a drop. I wanted you. I began to wonder, do you still feel as well as you tasted? Will the thickness of your pussy lips fit firmly around my penis? Remembering your pink pussy color and the curliness of your jet-black pussy hairs excited me. I realized this was the moment I waited for. I dreamt this very moment to life.

As my thoughts and memory grew of you, the harder my penis grew. With that, I knew I needed you near my body. I remembered your silky moans in the depths of my memory. I wanted you to ride me, to straddle me while wearing your pink, high-heel sandals. My vision was vivid, crystal clear. I knew what I wanted, and it was you. I wanted to carry you into the shower and love you all over the marble wall. The arch of your back would deepen with each stroke. With every motion, I would command that you love me as I love God. With your caramel behind slightly in the air, you would whisper in my ear, demanding that I love you, requesting that you be the only one I share this lovemaking with. The more the demands, the more strokes I threw at you. I awakened with you on my mind. When I pulled you closer to me, you enjoyed my control.

This morning, I awakened full of lust for you, and this evening, I went to bed in love with the thought of waking up next to you.

Sincerely yours,
KING

In Mary Jane's current situation, she pictured herself a mar to a true gentleman, unworthy of being respected. She felt like a blemish on her own skin.

Chapter 5
Bayo Conduilla

Teardrop stains covered her satin pillowcase. Hours were long and minutes were short. She blamed him and he blamed her. He burned her with a deep flame, while she burned him with the truth. She opened up, allowing him to see all of her, to accept her or leave her. He had not one question for her to answer. It made her damn near fear him with his silence. He just lay there. After taking him in her body and in her mouth, she thought he would have plenty to say. Yet, he had nothing.

Sweat rolled off of them. Heat poured between them. However, enough was not being said. She didn't know if she was good, bad, or indifferent. This secret love affair was taking all of her energy. Her husband! His wife! She wasn't able to deny her feelings for him, though. She was not able to stay away from this. She didn't mean to hurt the life that she hid. Yet, she chose to lie, cheat, and continue with this madness. Bittersweet. She was losing. Her heart chose to forget this was zip-less. Nothing was to matter. Time, condoms, hotel rooms, and silenced phones. That was it. No more. Tears showered her face.

He looked as if he wanted to say something, but chose to remain peaceful. She chose to lie, taking back the truth she had given to him. She wanted to build a wall of forgetfulness. Lying next to her, he needed to bury himself deep within her. Unable to desire anything less, she gave in, wanting him to take control of her body. She cradled the thought that she was more than ready to desire him the same. She desired his touch, his ability to hold her when the nights were dark and the sun hid behind the moon. The eclipse of lovemaking was upon them. She fought to believe she was stronger than the desire of their flesh.

His tongue went on a journey she was unable to handle. Starting with her tears, he wiped them away one lick at a time, ending at her chin. He kissed every freckle on her face. The ones behind her ears that refused to expose themselves, he found. Allowing her eyes to roll back, she surrendered to his sensual touches and the way he caressed her nipples with his teeth. They ached with pain and delectation. Leaving his marks, he claimed her.

The consequences did not alarm either of them. His sensuality continued far and wide. She cried out. She moaned. She jerked. He chivvied her body…pestering their souls, reminding her, working her. She called out his name, Ahmick Cane, hoping it would save her. He was unjustifiable. Their actions were indefensible. Unexplainable. His name meaning the strength of God's flock, she wanted to tell him that he was the strength of her body. She could see how he was the chosen child to lead her to freedom. Sexual freedom. His body covered her, loving her with his heated passion and desire. His body outweighed her. The power!

Tying her legs together with a silk Latin scarf, he climbed her torso. He became her body armor. Sliding his large penis in her mouth, a harmonic rhythm emerged with their movements. Taking him in was a task. She pulled it in deep with the suction of her throat. His waist grinded into her face, fucking it. She sucked and licked. She sucked his dick so hard that her cheeks began to sink in, causing dimples where none existed before. Pulling her hair up and away from her face, he choked her as he wrapped his hand around her larynx. She could not breathe. She gasped for air. The sounds released as muffles from her. Tears rolled. Moans erupted. She came. And she came again. She wanted more, but he needed his first. Sticking a finger inside herself, he became her sexual fan when nothing was possible.

They began to speak the Mandingo language, the language of West Africans, the warriors and strength of their land. The chief of their kingdom, he stood. Mandingo tall, sexy chocolate, thick, and sensual. His lips were a two-toned dark brown, and he had straight, pearly white teeth. Chunky shoulders. Strong forearms. Caring for her! Holding her! His laughter was her laughter. She inhaled him while he exhaled her. They were as one.

Time escaped them. Years in college, she was powerless to value the woman he wanted her to become. He dug deep inside her with his words. She wept for what was done. Their actions should have condemned them. His fingerprints were left on her skin. Flesh against flesh, he embedded himself in her. Lustful thoughts triggered guilty actions. His semen seeped from his ligament. She felt him touching and kissing deeper than surface pleasure. He kissed her soul. She smelled their sweat and mixture of passion. He spoke to her. Syllable by syllable, his words found their way into her heart.

"Grow with me," he said.

She didn't want to grow. At least not as this beast he desired. Loving him was a challenge. For him, having her was a joy. Instead of growing together, they allowed time to get away from them. The notion crossed their minds. Marriage, kids, a house that they would call their home. It all crossed their minds. Instead, on graduation day with degrees in hand, they shared a passionate goodbye kiss, promising to keep in touch. Doctrine in Psychology. Masters in Sociology. They were prepared for the professional world, but not for one another.

Kissing goodbye was her beginning, not her end. She boarded a plane to México. She rested there for a month. She thought about what could have been…what should have been. She wanted more. Incapable of fighting for more, she hid. She stayed still. She lay on the beaches, watching the waves climb the sand. She took classes on the language. She read a plentiful of books. She lost track of the different ways the sun would rise and fall on the land below. Time became unjust. She was unable to explain her reasoning for being there. She strived for all of her goals, and still, she had no reason for her actions. She was no longer tired. She was rested and mature enough to know it was time to go home.

Her last day in Mexico, she decided to enjoy more than the scenery. Up until then, she had chosen to be alone on an island full of exotic individuals. She ate, drank, and danced. Reaching intoxication was her initial thought. Her dress flowed away from her skin as if her body would prefer to be exposed to the darkness of the sky. The movements of her hips were inviting. She was inviting anyone who dared to approach her, anyone who could understand and appreciate her need for freedom. That night, she met him. She met her husband.

Loving him was not an option. She cared enough to try something different. They made eye contact. Weak, she looked away first. His seduction was erotic. From corner to corner, they worshipped their outer beings. His name she did not know. His career was not of concern. Only the intense moments that passed mattered.

More moments passed, and the more intense they became. Her dress ran its course over her body. While approaching her, he slowed his pace. She felt like she was cheating. Could there be someone at home waiting for her? She was wrong; they had let go. They had said their goodbyes. Waking up the next morning, she would be alone. She refused to let that happen.

She watched his chest as his muscles contracted in and out. His triceps rotated while he stretched. She was unsure if he was even coming towards her. However, he traveled to his own tempo. His movements stimulated her. That alerted her. She was used to attention. Her natural charm had always worked in her favor.

She thought to herself, *My name is Bayo…Bayo Conduilla.* She heard herself speaking to him, talking to him, laughing with him. The precise moment he arrived in front of her, she became more aware of his beauty. The dark complexion of his brawn covered his skeleton perfect. This allowed each muscle to protrude through, giving the idea that he was capable of protecting her.

Simply reaching for her hand, his first statement to her was, "May I ask your name?" He spoke with such gentleness.

"Bayo Conduilla," she responded.

His expression shocked her. So, she generously went into the details of her name, a name chosen by her mother's best friend. Its origin belonged to her father's family. They are Nigerian. It means to find joy. Conduilla is her mother's maiden name, which meant, "with Him we shall prosper". Together, it means in order to find joy we must prosper with Him. As a child, she did not understand the power of her name. Her mother made sure to tell her that she found her joy with birthing pains.

She felt herself talking and doing no listening. So, she asked him, "What's your name?"

"Abdullah Brick," he replied.

Curious, she smiled, wondering if his name had a meaning, as well.

He smiled and said, "Slave of sex God."

Before thinking, she jumped. Not sure what he meant, she gave him a puzzled look.

"Understand me," he continued. "My name means slave of sex God. My father was truly in love with my mother's sex. The way she had a way of making love to him over the phone controlled him. The way she called his name to wake him in the morning. My father loved every inch of her—her mind, body, and soul. When she became pregnant with me, her glow forced him into a deeper level of love for her. On the fifth anniversary of my birth, she passed, leaving me to love him as she had. Unconditionally! She was all that was left on earth to carry on with part of her flesh. Due to the depth of their love, he changed his name to Abdullah Brick. He was his proof that she once lived with him. Her scent still consumes the bed he lies in waiting for her."

Unable to move or respond appropriately, she stood in shock. Silence was upon them, and it was not uncomfortable. He lightened the mood by offering her a drink. Not interested in alcohol, she decided to offer him a walk so they could get to learn each other. She cherished the act when he braided his fingers through her right hand and guided her down the white sandy beaches. The sun set on the beginning of their conversation.

He was there on vacation, as was she. Thirty years old, he needed a change before change came to take his livelihood from him. An only child and after years of caring for his father, he desired to care for himself. He hated to admit that he regrettably put his father in an assistant living home. On the other hand, he admired his father, who fought as long as he could.

While Abdullah was a child, giving up on life was a difficult task for his father. As he grew older, his father gave up more and more with each birthday. When he turned eighteen, his father handed him a cherry wood box filled with memorabilia of his mother, including pictures of them as a family at the hospital. Stamped on the back of the photos was the date June 3rd, which was two days after his birth. He was surprised to see the joy in his father's eyes. The life still lived in him. His father was a man of his word. In every picture, his father was caressing her arms while she cradled her newborn. They were the trio that survived the deepest of misunderstandings. His mother had been told she would never be able to conceive, and his father's childhood convinced him that he would never have a family of his own. Abdullah believed his father finding his mother was his first blessing. Trusting her was a new blessing. Conversations would bring forth the truth. His father remembered his mother giving him one reason to love her. She said to him, "The only reason why you should love me is because I love you. If for not that reason alone, love me when loving me is right." As his father told him the story, he could see the glimmer in his father's eyes. Loving her was not a duty or a challenge. It was an offering he accepted.

In all the time of talking with Abdullah, she did not find herself bored. His life was interesting. Love in his world was a necessity. It was to be complete or not at all. Honest. Trustworthy. They spoke about determination, if she wanted to have children, their chosen careers, and their reasons for being in the land of exotic food and erotic people. They even spoke on the loved ones they decided to leave behind and why.

His reason was a simple one. He left her because she refused to comprehend and be fair-minded of the love he had for his father and how he refused to let go of him. She wanted Abdullah to allow his father to waste away in a nursing home, while he, on the other hand, wanted to cherish his father's life. In the end, she got her way. Somehow, she did not see she would lose him the same. His reasons were more difficult than hers.

She explained about their college love and how it died before the ending of school. They became…she became bored. Their sex was typical and she thought he deserved more. She also believed his appetite was more than she could handle. It started with porn. Then strip clubs, lap dances, and making movies outdoors. The more she gave into his fantasies, the less she liked herself. She felt disrespected. Never once did they discuss marriage until she began to complain. She wanted him to desire her as a complete woman, not a toy. She grew bored with him. The sex was interesting. Making her an honest woman was a different story, though. So, she chose to leave the man who she once gave her all to. Besides school and work, he was her being. That bothered her. She left. Though it was scary at first, she was proud of herself.

Chapter 6
The Touch

    The sun began to rise over the ocean. The shimmering yellow, gold, and purple reflected in their eyes. Watching him watch her, she wanted him to reach out and touch her skin. She wanted him to pull her close to his chest. Instead, he rubbed her forearms, sending chills up the rest of her arm. She smiled. She yearned for more. She yearned for the colors to stay with her, to cover them like a blanket covers a bed. She wanted him to climb between the colors and her. They loved the heat of the sun.

    She pulled him closer to her. She tugged until he had no chance to deny her or say goodbye. Wanting him, she took control of the atmosphere, becoming assertive, strong, and bigheaded. Going with the rhythm of life, he allowed her to wrap herself inside of him. His skin was warm and caused her skin to tingle with joy. She shivered. The breeze became warmer. The heat between her thighs grew hotter as his manhood grew harder. She wondered did he know she knew he was fond of the attention she was giving him. She wanted to show him appreciation for his thoughts.

    She kissed the palms of his hands. Gliding her tongue against his lifeline, she followed it from beginning to end. She found her tongue circling his wrist. Nibbling on his fingertips, she watched his tongue caress his lips. He was enjoying what she was doing; she was enjoying pleasing him. Pulling her breasts out of her dress, she becalmed the deliberation. Lying back on the sand, she gave into the temptation. She moaned. Allowing the hairs on her neck to rise to the occasion, she gave him lead. Becoming submissive to the thought of a strong man, she gave in.

    His scent, which was strong and gentle, belonged to the Giorgio Armani family. He smelled of a gentleman. She was no longer her own best friend. Her fingers were no longer needed to linger inside of her to satisfy herself. Her disappointed fingers entangled themselves in her hair, rubbing her roots. Her fingertips found a new home during lovemaking. She pulled and tugged at her hair, while he kissed the hairs of her skin.

He wanted to pull and tug at he hair, as well, but instead, he whispered, "Call me when you need me. Call me when no one else satisfies your appetite for conversation."

He whispered until she could no longer make out the words he spoke.

6:30 a.m.

She wanted him to wait for her. She wanted to say yes. She wanted him to say no, to have better control. He watched her while she watched him. Their bodies began to converse. Her heart said, not today, but yoni refused to listen. She continued to indulge in her own wetness.

They should have been in a bed in one of their homes. Her legs jumped with each touch. This man was making love to her with no words. He talked to her soul. Pulled her into his grasp and did not let go.

She could not believe she had been so foolish. A woman of her word, she refused to believe he was typical. She let go. Her clothes were no longer hers to own. The sand below wore them. Wrapping her legs around his neck, he kissed her. She purred. Her pussy was his breakfast. Spreading her lips apart, his tongue wrapped itself on her clitoris. She called out, "Yes, yes, yes!" It was if the word no did not exist. She moaned, rolled her hips, and said yes again.

He had her speechless, restless, and motivated to cherish him the same. He had her right where he wanted her…in his mouth. She had waited for this. No extras. She was enough for his sexual appetite. They shared a world of speechless acts, just the way she liked it. Just the two of them as the sun continued to rise. Their footprints were not the only ones in the sand anymore. They had an audience. They were far and beyond, yet near enough to hear them. If they were to look in their direction, the spectators would have gotten jealous. She was curious why they ran in the opposite direction of such beauty. Their lovemaking should have been shared. It was unique. The more they manifested in one another's passion, the hotter the day became.

With the sun rising, they were unable to complete what they started, so they moved on to her suite. While showering, she watched his muscles again. They celebrated their union and ability to be honest with one another with hugs and kisses, not empty promises. She loved a man she barely knew. Dangerous! This thing called reality was difficult without love. She fell dangerously for this man. At that moment, he was all she had.

His body clung to her as if she was all he had. He was healing the pain that lay on her flesh. She allowed him to do so. The presence of lust was in the disguise of love. She didn't want to be without him another moment.

She took his dick inside of her. Riding him was joyous. He touched her back, calming her rhythm. He joined the beat that her hips made. Front, back, side to side. Front, back, side to side. They were alone. Recording actions with memories, she took mental notes to ride him like loving him was not new to her. He needed a woman like her, and she needed a man of his nature.

He took her hands in his, taking better control. He confronted her, slowing her down. Their bodies began to talk again—whispering sweet secrets to each other, calling each other, demanding each other's time and energy. Her heart raced past insanity. Her emotions were on a sporadic rollercoaster. This was wrong. This was fate. This was love.

She began apologizing to him, to herself, to her mind, body, and soul. This was not the way to eternal love. The sex never stopped, though. The conversation she had was completely for her own sanity. The words stayed within her while moans escaped her lips. The dip in her back curved into a question mark. She felt his dick in every area of her womanhood. Her walls cradled him as a newborn. Settling inside, he rode the clouds of softness to ecstasy. Working his hips against her body, he took control from the bottom and rolled her until he was on top. He pushed her legs in the air. Her knees were against the bed while her feet rested on his shoulders. He was getting what he came for, which was nothing but pure pleasure.

His eyes renewed themselves with each blink. He blinked to control the act of cumming inside her pussy walls. Each time his eyes closed, she contracted her muscles tighter. Not expecting her trivial performance, he came hard. Grabbing her throat, he lost control. She owned his semen. They were even. He loved her sex just like his father loved his mother, while she basked in the attention and affection. The heat climbed the walls of her suite, and sleep soon crept from their pores.

Chapter 7
The Plane Ride Home

She was going home to a homecoming. She could only imagine her family's reaction. Afraid she would not come home, her mother called continuously. Her mother believed she had wasted time in college just to become a storeowner. She did not understand that sometimes a person needs a chance to breathe before starting a new journey in their life. She was going home with a bronzed tan, a husband, and a chance to kill her mother when she announced, "I'm married." She did not fear her, but she did not want to hurt her either.

He transferred his job to San Francisco, California. She would move there because it was the closest to both of their homes. They married without concern for what anyone thought but themselves. His one request was that they remained close enough to his father. She honored that. Staying close to her family was not a problem. They were spread across the state of California. Some were even in Tucson, Arizona, of all places. It was crowded and hot as ever there. The water was not fresh, recycled actually; and the temperate would reach ninety degrees in December. She smiled at the thought. Remembering going through the list of possible cities, they scratched it off first.

Looking out the small window to her left, she watched the plane glide above the clouds below. The attendant placed the phone receiver back in its cradle after giving the passengers instructions. Buckling her seatbelt, she prayed. Landing was not her favorite part of flying.

Abdullah must have sensed her discomfort, because he whispered, "Relax. You are no longer alone."

She took one gasping breath, closed her eyes, and laid her head on his shoulder. This time, she thanked God for her blessing. He was on time.

Once they disembarked the plane, she saw signs welcoming her home held high in the air. Her mom, dad, brother and rest of her family must have thought she came bearing gifts. The only gift she came with was the blessing she received, the gift of her husband. Their screams and smiles lessened when they noticed him. While they stood there confused, she was happy.

Hand in hand, her and her husband walked towards the mob of family waiting for her. She left with the idea of making some changes in her life. That she did. Walking towards them, she could smell the fear in Abdullah's heart. He had no idea what to think. She tried to warn him that tons of questions were to come, most of them being from her mother until the rest of the family followed her lead and joined in. She had called ahead to tell her mother that she had something to share with the family, which explained why everyone was there at the airport awaiting her arrival.

Standing in front of them became cold and awkward. She received hugs and kisses. Yet, they did not say one word to him. The warmness she was used to seeing from her family was absent. They were distant, almost fearful like. It seemed the kids were the only ones who hadn't lost their manners. When she introduced him as her husband, the air became so thick that she forgot she was an adult. They appeared disappointed, hurt even. She was in dismay. She lost hope that they would understand her feelings as to why she chose to have him before they met him.

During the ride home, they opened up. His hellos were finally answered, and their line of questioning began. *Where is your family from? What do you do for a living? How old are you? What does your name mean?* She smiled, happy that things were going in the right direction. They were making him uncomfortable, but for the right reasons. They needed to get to know him so they could come to love him just as she had.

Once they arrived at her parents' home, it became clear to her the miscommunication. Her mother had her attention while she relieved herself. As she peed, she spoke with assuredness.

"I knew you would come back home married. I wanted you to come back married because that's what you wanted. You wanted to be someone's wife, to have that part of your life completed.

Somehow, I thought you would marry someone we know. Hell, even someone you know."

She was upset for all the wrong reasons. *I do know him,* she thought to herself. Trying to convince her mother of that would have been a waste of time. Besides, she was ready to go home. So, her mother's interrogation would have to wait until she was no longer tired or hungry.

As she finished washing her hands, there was a knock on the door. To her surprise, it was not her dad. Thank goodness, because their bathroom was not big enough for the both of them and the entire trauma. Instead, it was her brother, who stood there as if he was King Kong stuck in a net. He appeared ill, sick to his stomach. Her brother was upset. Not for any obvious reasons.

"What's the matter with you?" she asked him.

"Besides you running off and getting married without your family," he snapped.

"Well, yes, other than that!"

"Oh yeah, other than your husband and your ex talking in the living room right now? No, there's nothing wrong."

"What the hell are you talking about?"

"Mom knew you were coming home, and somehow, she thought it would be a good idea to invite him over for a homecoming dinner," he replied with a chuckle.

At that point, the misunderstanding at the airport became clear to her. Her mother had the idea of playing matchmaker. She didn't know what to do. She turned slowly to her right, wanting to ask her what the hell, but the words did not come. She refused to run out the door. She was nervous, fearful, and most of all, embarrassed. She had just broken up with him a month ago. She wanted him to leave; this was family time. He decided for the both of them that they were not a family. He gave her walking papers. Handed her the keys to her apartment and walked away as if what they had meant nothing. She thought it was her that he would lay next to after a long night at the office. Either way, the more she thought about it, the stronger she got.

Turning away from her mother and eldest brother, she walked into the living room, kissed her husband, and then acknowledged her ex. It was simple. She apologized to Ahmik for not being there to introduce him to her husband Abdullah. They shook hands and both responded, "No worries." They were two small words, but they bothered her. Same words spoken at the same time! They shouldn't have been that similar in thoughts. Yet, they were.

Ahmik erupted with laughter. "Excuse my manners. This is my fiancée Aba Harrison."

Her heart stopped. How dare he? This was a homecoming for her, and he had the nerve to bring a fucking date. Her eyes told on her.

"Baby, are you okay?" Abdullah asked.

She had been in the mood to eat, but she most definitely lost her appetite at that time. Shaking her hand sent chills up her arm and down her spine. Her face was familiar. Maybe she wanted her to be familiar so she could know what it was about her that was so different from her. How long had he known her? Were they together when she and him were together? So many questions, but she had no right to ask him a damn thing.

She had to walk away. Having her entire family watching her personal life unfold in front of her was not fair or comfortable. She reached for Abdullah's hand, looked at her family, and apologized for being so tired, but they had to turn in. Her excuse was easy; jet lag was kicking in.

As she grabbed her keys out of the kitchen and headed for the garage, she heard her father in the distance. He was a man of few words. He spoke soft and only spoke when he felt it was needed. His footsteps grew closer as the garage door rose. He walked over to Abdullah and rubbed his shoulder, welcoming him into the family.

"Tomorrow will be better," Abdullah told her.

Walking over to the driver side of her Hummer, he hugged her while offering no words. He allowed her to linger in his arm like a newborn. She wanted to express herself about her mother's actions, but he simply said, "Tomorrow."

The day was coming to an end when they got on the highway heading south on I-35. They rode in silence. She wanted to say something, but nothing came out. He rubbed her. His actions were always on time.

It's okay. We're okay. No matter what happens tomorrow, I want him to know all of my love is for him. I chose him when the night turned into day. There is nothing or no one who could replace the love I have for him. Every moment of every day I will continue to love him. Our plans are ours and no one else's, she thought, convincing herself.

Arriving home, he carried her over the threshold. He still honored her despite knowing her reaction to Ahmik having a fiancée was dead wrong. But, like he said, tomorrow would be better.

Shower and loving her husband together on their first night at home was not what she wanted it to be. She needed to write. She needed to get a few things off her mind. Instead, she ignored her thoughts and lulled him to sleep. Making love was not in their plans. His arms wrapped around her, one on her waist and another around her neck. Their legs were entwined, toes against toes. With knees locked in place, she fell asleep.

Awakening to the sound of her alarm clock the next morning, she found herself still unsure of what she wanted to do about her true feelings. Sliding away from Abdullah, she felt deceitful, but she needed to write. She needed to get those thoughts off her chest. So, she grabbed her journal and crawled on the couch. Cornering herself, she thought, *How do I feel? What am I willing to write down that will not cause the truth to hurt too badly?* She started with the topic "Unsure", but she changed it to "I Wanted You".

I wanted you. You were my vision when the nights were dark. I cared for you before I knew you. Holding you in my arms and kissing you goodnight was merely a dream. I loved you and I was your pawn. I gave you a joke, and you handled me fragilely. I needed you to use your smartness to love me. Clever thoughts to use on me were in your plan. You were my all and I was your fall. You blamed me when the wind blew south. You chained me when the rain poured down. When the sun shined, you allowed its rays to tickle my true thoughts of you. Confused! I wanted you.

I needed you. I needed you to save me and raise me. I was your blessing while you wanted to dress me and shave me. I wanted freedom out of your disguised kingdom. I was imprisoned with lust, control, and hope. All this time I was truly your joke. Your smiles are fake, making it more than I can take. I wanted you, or did you need me? Who fulfills who? When I'm not home, do you enjoy a quiet walk? Or do you ring my phone to no end, asking and begging for my return? If I were to leave, what would you do with yourself? I saved you. In return, you're killing me. Killing me softly! Dragging my soul slowly through the depths of the valley and over the peaks of the highest mountain, you are killing me.

We were different. We dared each other to love when love seemed impossible. I honored your challenge to stand for the both of us in front of the ones we love. I may have wanted you, but you needed me. You needed me to wash you, shoulder you, catch every tear that fell towards the land we call earth. The dirty brown ground we build homes on, your tears made it possible for the grass to grow tall on. You flooded these sandy roads with the tears and fears that you continue to blame me for. I asked for optimistic ways; you laughed. You said I was a fool to dare say those words to you. Now I have the same tears, the same fears. I now cry at night the same tears you cried on my shoulder. Difference is I am forced to do it alone. I blame you for my trust issues. My insecurities! All of these things should tackle your dreams and shock you in your sleep. Choke breath out of your lungs. Death should have been knocking on your door. Headache, migraine, heartache, chest pain, and more should interrupt your world, as they do mine. When you see me, laugh as you did in my arms while I cradled you to sleep.

I need you! I need you to grow as the man on the moon. Unseen! I want you to shine as the stars in the sky. Too bright to stare at. Walk past me as a stranger in the land of the free. Allow me to be the woman you dared me not to be. With my wide hips, strong back, and long feet, allow me to be just me! Because I wanted you when the nights were dark, I no longer have a heart for you. All because I wanted you!

She wrote those words, shocking herself. So deep in her own thoughts, she did not hear the shower running. She did not notice him standing behind her holding a cup of Joe. He was able to cherish her while allowing her to grow as a woman. Running her hair through his fingers, she was able to find comfort in his fingertips. She relaxed. As she laid her journal down, he walked around to the front of the couch. Resting his feet on the coffee table, he asked what they should plan for the celebration of their union. Wondering where that came from, she smiled and asked what would be ideal for him.

Then she expressed, "I would like it to be small with close friends and family."

They agreed it should stand out the box because their union was not typical. Therefore, loving each other in front of their friends and family had to be the same.

Overexcited she screamed, "Masquerade ball! A black and white masquerade ball!"

He was just as excited with her suggestion. They decided on black masks for the men and white masks with large feathers for the women. Their first dance song would be Jaheim's "The Chosen One". The song would fade in and they would find each other, their way of choosing each other in front of everyone. Making their way to the middle of the dance floor, they would love each other, moving to their own beat. After the first course, everyone would then have to find their companion, move to the middle of the floor, and dance. The more they planned, the more excited she became.

He was ready for breakfast. She offered to cook. Instead, he wanted her to take a shower. He wanted to cater to her. When she went into their bedroom, she found he had lit every candle. Her black, silk housecoat lay on the bed. He had found her white satin thong trimmed in pink, with the matching bra. Steam filled the air from the running shower. The aroma of fresh vanilla cranberry crept from under the door. He had sprayed the tub floor with bubbles just for the scent. The lights were out, and three candles lit the way. Speechless, she moved the shower curtain and stepped in. The heat was more than arousing. Facing the water, she stood there while it ran over her shoulders and down her back.

His intentions to honor her as his wife were beautiful. She wanted to share this with him. She wanted him to see her joy. The pleasure he gave her, she wanted to share with him. She wanted him to know she was going nowhere. Letting him go was not an option. The attention was wonderful.

The heat became near unbearable, steadily filling the air within the bathroom. It filled her lungs. Inhaling and exhaling became a challenge. As if sensing she could no longer take this peaceful moment, her husband stepped in with a cup of cool water and poured it down her back. Chills ran over her body. He began kissing away the chills on her earlobes. Down her neck, his lips followed her spine. Stopping at her tailbone, his lips found a home. Continuing down the back of her thighs, his lips stopped to rest on the back of her knee.

Spreading her legs apart, he inserted two fingers into her yoni, moving them in and out. He played her body like a guitar, stroking every string and causing a new tune to erupt out of her. The more he played her body, the more her legs began to shake. She shook uncontrollably. She came and came some more until it dripped down his hand and arm. Her leg wrapped around his gave him more access to the depths of her yoni.

Her husband was enjoying the idea of loving her when no one else could. He chose her, while she chose to enjoy the very thing she needed the most. She needed him not to give up on her. Showering in a candle-lit bathroom, she laughed in his arms and cried at the thought that it would all have to end. They would have to get out of the shower, dry off, and dress to go to her mother's home to be interrogated. She wanted to refuse. She wanted them to stay in bed and ignore the door and phone calls when they reached out to bother them. Instead, her husband wanted them to confront all the questions. He wanted to laugh with his new family. He felt dealing with her family would be a lot easier than dealing with his father alone. She moaned at his ability to calm her, to control and read her thoughts. Looking her husband in his eyes, she gave farewell to the unsure thoughts of loving and marrying him. He was her new comfort zone.

Dressed and ready to go, he drove them up I-35.

Chapter 8
Lost Kamel

Thinking back, she was unable to recall the emotions. Yet, it seemed she could remember every movement his hands made and every word he spoke to her. Sitting here today, she honestly had to recall from a recessed area deep within. She figured she would start where her memory was best. However, looking back, there was always the thought of wishing she would have taken the ride offered, but that was then. She couldn't go back and change the past.

It was pouring down rain in Seattle, Washington, where her family lived for most of her childhood. They lived in the Central District before it became the CD. Coming from where they had been, their lake view was more than most could enjoy. Her mother returned to college when she was still in diapers and became a prominent businesswoman. Whenever her mother saw opportunity, she leaped at it. It was her new spiriting career, from one thing to the next.

Once they arrived in Tacoma, Washington, at nine o'clock in the evening, she knew they had found their home. There was nothing that could stop her from succeeding. Their first stop was the ocean. They had been on the road for three days, and the first thing she wanted to touch was the water. She said she needed to smell the salt from the water. So, they drove another hour and a half. They materialized the drive; it was a vision worth waiting for once they arrived.

The car hadn't come to a complete stop before she and her brother opened the doors and took off running toward the ocean as fast as they could. Her mother, on the other hand, walked. She gracefully accepted the challenge ahead. As a young girl, she could not understand her purpose for walking when anyone with sight could see how excited she was for being offered the chance at a new life.

It was her twelfth grade year of high school. She was the co-captain of the cheerleading squad. The gold and green uniform was the best thing she had going that year. With the end of the year coming, her squad made plans to have a block party in the gym. It was a tradition. The late night hours were to be expected. The teachers and the school in general were excited for the classmates, the twelfth graders. They were given less stressful homework. The test days would come and they would rush through. Afterwards, they hurried themselves to the gym to finish the decorations. With a week left to finish, they were given permission to have one late night, one last night to produce a grand finale. Five hours after the last class was dismissed, three hours after the tutors left, and one hour before the janitors made it to the floor to remind them of their time left, it was then that they discovered the beauty of teamwork.

That year, they wanted to have a 70's theme; the bell-bottoms, big hair, and hippie movement. Large black and white photos were posted everywhere. They pushed for historical signs to show how the country as a whole had grown from the Civil Rights movement, the GLBT movement, women's movement, the ending of segregation in the south, and more. By the time they finished that night, they were exhausted, had paper cuts, were sweaty, and starving. The sandwiches their parents had donated for the cause were gone.

She called her mother to let her know she needed a ride home since she was grounded from driving her car because she was caught giving a ride to a friend her parents didn't know. That was the golden "rule". Before someone could be in her car, she had to introduce that person to her mother or stepfather first. The way her mother enforced that rule, it should have been a law.

That evening, she waited for her mother in front of the building until the rain started coming down sideways. The sight of him was a joy because she knew she wouldn't have to stand outside in that mess. Everyone in the school knew him as helpful, genuine, and caring. He was not the typical janitor. He didn't smell; he drove a nice car; and he was very polite. He cared about the building and it showed.

While walking up to her, he asked, "Do you want to wait inside of the doorway?"

Since the rain had started to come down even harder, she accepted his offer and called a friend from the squad to talk with her while she waited. They talked about the dance, the show, and all the great things they had experienced since freshman year. Tonya asked her if she wanted her to turn around and come get her. She paused, giving it some thought, but her mother would have pissed a fit if she came all the way to the school to get her and she was gone. She would have called her, but she didn't answer the phone while driving, and especially not when it's raining. So, she declined the ride and, from the inside looking out, lurked over the rain falling.

The scent of Pleasure men cologne smacked her hard. It was a handsome smell, the kind that made a person smile because it was relaxing. The man grabbed her from behind before she had a chance to turn around. Her hands were then secured behind her back with some type of restraint, making it impossible for her to free herself. She cried out for help, but he ignored her. He continued to steal her innocence. As she fought him with every ounce of her strength, they rocked and rolled over the small area of the hallway. After he finished, he wiped her with a damp towel and then helped her to her feet. He pulled her pants up on her waist. He fixed her hair as if she was a newborn. She had become a woman without consulting her Heavenly Father. She was angry. She was angry at the world and angry with her mother for not being there to save her. As he continued to smooth down her hair, he spoke. She didn't recognize the scent, but the voice came from someone who she looked up to like a father.

"No one will believe you, so keep it to yourself," he whispered.

She was terrified. She could still feel his penis growing within her. It pressed against the walls of her vagina. She remembered the stretching was painful. The more she fought against him, the stronger his will became and the harder his penis grew. She was damaged from the inside out. She was numb from head to toe. His statement confirmed that he was worried about her talking, while she was more concerned about the simple task of walking. Everything was sore; her skin ached from the touch of her clothing. Tears filled her eyes once more, and deafness covered her ears. She experienced a crawling sensation on her skin that was unknown to her.

He woke her from the nightmare with a kiss on her cheek. He tapped her on the shoulder and said, "Your mother is here." She could hear everything he said, but her feet would not move. She felt as though she was running in place. He gave her a slight shove towards the door. She figured that's what got her moving. She must have taken a minute too long, because her mother started to blow the horn.

When she finally stopped running, her body had escaped the rain but not the pain. She couldn't ever imagine such disappointment in her superiors. Her mother talked about things she could not understand. The words floated around her. With air seizing from her lungs, she fought to hold back the tears. She fought to remain intact. She fought to suppress the anger, fear, and doubt she held inside her.

Somehow, the will of the truth was stronger than her lie. She began to scream, yelling for her mother to stop the SUV. The tears flowed from her as she began to experience a warm sensation in her pants. Thinking she was having an accident, she told her mother that she was peeing on herself. The thought disgusted her.

Her mother looked at her with a beaming look in her eyes and said, "You're probably just getting your period."

Up until then, she hadn't given it much thought about never having had a period yet. The stream of water came harder from her eyes, and she dropped her head into her hands.

"Mr. Johnson, the principal, raped me in the hall," she blurted out. "He tied my hands behind my back and raped me on the floor."

Her mother slammed on the brakes, and the truck slid a few feet before coming to a complete stop. She turned on the interior lights, and that's when she saw the fear written across her face. She hurried and called the police, her stepfather, her uncles, and any other male she could think of to call. It seemed her mother dialed the numbers faster when she realized her daughter was bleeding.

With her bleeding heavily, her mother drove with an urgency that she had never seen before to get to the emergency room. She fought against rain, wind, and thunder. She drove like she was fighting the devil himself.

How do I breathe after the true essence of my soul has been ripped from my body? she thought.

Her youth had been destroyed before it was hers to give away. Someone should have been there. He stole her innocence.

"Where were you? What took you so long?" she asked her mother.

Just as fast as the words came out of her mouth, she regretted it. She was blaming her mother, when she was not the one to blame. The English language couldn't express in words the look her mother had on her face in that moment.

When they arrived at the hospital, the hospital ran tests, drew blood, and gave her a swab test to check for semen. They asked if he had used a condom and wanted her to provide a description of him. They wanted to know how she knew him and why she was at school so late alone. The questions came at her like fastballs being thrown by a professional pitcher. They would not slow down. They demanded for her to respond quickly, not understanding she was still in shock. They showed no compassion for what she was going through.

That night when she left the hospital with her family, who had flooded the emergency room waiting area, she took a bath and then a shower. The truth seeped in as she washed her body; she fell against the shower wall. Flashes of his belt around her wrists broke her spirit, causing her to crawl out of the shower.

She was grateful she was the last girl he was able to successfully harm in such a manner. He was found guilty six months after the incident. She often wondered did he look at himself in the mirror and see the images of him controlling her arms and legs while forcing his tongue in her mouth and down her neck?

Thoughts and actions that should have been pleasurable gave her bad chills when it was time for her to explore the opposite sex. During that time in her life, uncontrollable tears often welled up in her eyes. Her goals were unattainable without her inspiration. It was lost; she was lost. She was hopeful and hopeless at the same time. It seemed impossible. Yet, that was the attitude she feared more than the thought of it happening to someone else. It hurt and burned her up not to blame him anymore. However, she made the choice that if she was going to be the woman she was born to be, she had to let it go.

She never forgot what happened that night, but today, she remembers why she is here. She knows she is the best person for the Jojoba Essence journey for surviving women. This is where she is supposed to be, a sorority of beautiful women from different tracks of life. Carrying the torch of freedom for the next generation of Jojoba Essence women is a true test of her survivor skills.

Chapter 9
Twelve Inches Deep

Twelve inches of fake flesh unattached to spirit, mind, or body. It was her manhood. Not what one would prefer, but she needed to climax. She needed to scream sweet Jesus. Calling his name in satisfaction was the beginning as she rolled her hips over him. Grabbing her sheets, she needed him. She needed him inside her womanhood. Giving into her need to purge her body of all the pinned up stress, she inserted her twelve inches of flesh. *The act of catharsis!* She had him pressed firmly against her flesh. Deep inside of her, she pushed and pulled him. The tip of her man played with her clitoris. He tickled her and she curled her toes.

He tickled her until she called out, "Bae…bae…bae…baby, I'm cum…I'm cumming."

Talking to her manhood, she moaned for him. He hummed her name. He hummed a simple song. He made commands for her to cum for him. He needed to know his magic was more than a battery. He was man. He was a man in his own right. Her crying out to him came naturally. She desired his strength. His ability to please her was not only adored, but also adorable. He was the master of her livelihood. She was unable to move another muscle.

She awakened to the sound of her alarm clock at 6:30 a.m. Turning over to hit the button to stop the annoying sound, she was confused. She couldn't remember when she fell asleep. With Mr. Man next to her, she pulled herself out of bed. It was morning and she had to jog. She started this health kick during her graduate year of college.

Experiencing PTS (pussy tragic stress), she was close to her own death. She toyed with the idea of getting a toy, even went to a few parties, but she refused to indulge. So, instead, she started to run. She ran so much that running became her life. Before class, after class, and during class, she would look up new paths on the school website in order to experience different views of the romantic city while jogging. After about two months, she was tired of running and her PTS remained. That's when she challenged herself to walk into an adult store uptown. She won the bet, but not before disguising herself with a scarf and large black sunglasses. She was horny and a freak, but didn't want anyone else to know.

After entering the store, she traveled down aisle one that had shelves filled with candles, organic smoking products, and costumes for both sexes. The aisles seemed to go on for nearly a mile. Maybe that's how she felt because it was her first time in such an establishment.

With the neon lights flashing outside, one would have thought it was packed with people. But, except for a few people milling about, it was empty. There was an older couple looking to rekindled the fire that once burned between the two of them, a guy who seemed out of place while standing next to the free coffee stand, and a young woman, who appeared to know exactly what she wanted, stood at the end of the aisle. With confidence, the strange woman walked down aisle three, stopped at the first row of movies, and grabbed two of them. She was unable to make out the titles. She watched anyway. She was strong in her ability to express her sexuality. After leaving aisle three, she walked over to aisle five, which was where she needed to be. It had all types of toys varying in length, width, and color. They even had toys that you could program to say your name and certain things you like to hear while pleasuring yourself.

That mysterious woman must have sensed she was following her, because she looked back. When she did, she dropped her head, ashamed that she needed a stranger's guidance to open her eyes to sexual healing. She stopped near the videos where she once stood and picked up *Pimps Up and Hoes Down, Volume 12*. To avoid eye contact with her, she studied the cover of the case. It had multiple pictures of women and a man in multiple positions and with various objects used as sex toys. The pictures alone turned her on. In the corner of the disc's case were the words "Featuring Mr. Man". Unsure which of the men on the cover was Mr. Man, she looked closer and saw a picture of an adult toy named after him. From the way every woman pictured was kissing him, licking him, and sucking on him, she figured they were really enjoying him or just some great actresses. She decided to purchase the movie AND the toy, which set her back a little over one hundred and twenty-two dollars.

Walking out of that adult store, she was more nervous than when she walked in. This time, though, she was nervous for herself. Her PTS would be taken care of, but would she be able to handle what he had to offer? He was twelve inches long and two inches thick. She figured he would dominate her.

She didn't remember the lady who freed her from her sexual entrapment until it was too late. When she had finally looked up from the case and made it to the cashier, the mysterious lady was nowhere in sight. Looking back, she was her hero. If she were to ever meet her, she would smile in confidence.

Driving down the boulevard, the traffic was light. Catching all of the green lights gave her the feeling that it was going to be a good day. She had been prepared to go running, but unfortunately, the thunder and lightning changed those plans. She made the decision not to allow yesterday's PTS to get in the way. PTS was no longer a problem since Mr. Man had done his job. He awakened senses that had gone numb after few weeks of no attention.

Running to escape the rain, she dashed into the main office. As the boss, she naturally got attention in a company that was made up of 432 employees. Having a low turnover rate, most seemed to appreciate the vision she had with her company. She and her sister Lolita decided to start a gossip column, which over the years had grown to become Never, Inc.

They had a small, hot-off-the-press newspaper. With that, they had an urban publication that highlighted upcoming urban storytelling men and women, who offered hope to the hopeless and dreams to the restless. People began embracing their way of life instead of cursing what came natural to them. They felt a part of their neighborhood. They began reading the stories written to establish family values, social roles, and participation in the community. More importantly, they were able to relate to what they were reading. They began to mimic the things they read about. Twenty years later and after twelve unbelievable New York bestsellers, they were happy. They didn't take their business from its home in Louisiana. She was a Louisianan at heart. She gave to her community and built others up.

As she walked throughout the office, her employees looked at her different. She started getting this vibe, as if everyone knew her secret of having devoured in sensual healing last night. She spoke with a smile, not demanding and commanding everyone. She was a pleasure to deal with and even more of a pleasure to look at. She entered the restroom to take a look in the mirror. She smiled. She loved herself.

While exiting the restroom, she bumped into the deliveryman. There he was right in front of her, apologizing for something she had done to him. He was her Mr. Man. She imagined him in between her sheets at night. She watched him carry those boxes as if he was carrying her to his castle. His frame stood five-nine. She had no idea of his weight, but he was muscular. He had silver blue eyes. His ears were even sexy to her. Starting with his back, she wanted her tongue to run all over his body. She wanted to caress his shoulders with her breasts. Just when she thought she could not think of anything different, she wanted this man twelve inches deep inside her. She wanted him to carry her on his shoulders. She wanted all of her womanhood in his mouth. She wanted him to enjoy the aroma of her strawberry-scented splash lotion.

Mentally, she wanted him to cure her of the mental abuse she indulged in every time she saw him. She wanted him to save her mind from the torched thoughts of his skin against her dampened flesh. She needed him to free the trapped thoughts of them making love against the elevator door.

Just when she thought she needed nothing else from him and desired nothing more of his flesh, he ran his working hand across her back. With that simple touch, she awakened from a deep daydream. She moaned to herself at the smell of this man. Walking by him was a challenge she was not up for. She allowed his presence to help balance her thoughts while he walked past her. He took one look back, asked was she okay, and then continued on. It would be seven days and a million thoughts before she would see his beauty again.

Getting past that brief moment of insanity, she strolled into her office without a care in the world. Red folder on her desk, she remembered the disunity of yesterday was still lingering. After sitting down, she rolled her neck around to relax her muscles and jumped right in. Calling the involved parties into her office, they were surprised at her actions. Once they came in, she absorbed all the information and made a decision. No write-ups. No extra supervision. And no reason to believe they would be interested in having extramarital intercourse in the closets anymore.

They were shocked to find out people knew what they were doing. Their coworkers kept their secrets for months. PTS captivated her being, and she lost control. Her anger enraged her. A brisk walk came upon her, and she was in their faces. Handing them a slip to meet her in the office at ten o'clock a.m., they were confused with her actions. She was furious with them. Not because they were cheating on their spouses or having sex in the workplace. No, she was upset because they were able to find one another. They would not allow anything or anyone to take away from their burning flesh. The fire that ran through their skin, veins, and sexual organs was an untamed fire that needed to be dealt with. The passion between them was one that she understood. Since her fire had been hosed down the previous night, she was able to understand the cool, relaxing feeling they felt when it was all done. Besides their embarrassment, guilt from their adultery was killing them slowly. They would have to go home and deal with reality. Stay or go? Live life with that burning desire or satisfy the need of their flesh? Those were questions they would have to ask themselves.

After that meeting, she felt relieved. She had punished myself enough with her approach to the situation and had gratitude for their response.

Moving throughout the day, things fell into place. The latest short story, *The Birth of Beefy's Pup,* had been published in the evening paper that was on its way to the newsstands. They were proud to say it was their first children's book, and it turned out to be a success. Kids loved it, and the school district used it to teach responsibility. They were building their communities and making them stronger. The community and those who inhabited the homes, grocery stores, coffee shops, and schools were their audience. They started at home with the parents. Just as the parents fell in love with reading to their children, the children fell in love with the attention they received from their parents. They were truly proud.

At the end of the day, she was swamped with calls. Someone

needed a job and reporters wanted an interview. She desired a stiff Cognac on the rocks. Six in the evening, she stopped answering calls. She sent home those who wanted to leave. While sitting in her office, time slipped by. Eight o'clock had come and gone. She needed to eat. Slipping on her gold-shimmering flats, she walked down the four flights of stairs, picking up her pace on the last two flights. She didn't get a chance to run that morning. Therefore, she wanted to put in as much movement as she could. After such a hard day of work, she desired a candle-lit dinner. She craved lobster, crab, and cheddar biscuits. She wanted Red Lobster.

While walking down the alley toward her car, it became eerily quiet. She was walking with caution, when she heard a muffled sound that could have been her name. She took soft steps toward the sound. Newspaper rustled in the distance. She was more than scared; she was terrified. She became uneasy and concerned at the sight of the man lying in a shallow pool of blood and his life barely holding on. She began to scream; she lost her cool. Forgetting to call for help, she ran in circles. Thirty seconds later, she held her phone in her hand dialing 9-1-1. It was coming to her. Where she was and who he was. He was her masculine, handsome deliveryman. Someone had stabbed him. That was clear.

Once they arrived at the hospital, she was only privileged with a small amount of information until his family came. He had been stabbed twelve times. He was mugged, and he would have been a victim of homicide if she hadn't left work when she did.

Sitting, pacing, strolling the halls of the hospital, she became restless while waiting for his family. She did not know who was coming. She was informed a woman was listed as his emergency contact. That made her fearful. Not knowing if it was his wife, friend, sister, or mother, she wanted to run. Instead, she waited. She wanted them to know everything she knew.

An hour later, a nurse approached with a woman walking next to her. Once they reached where she was standing, the nurse began explaining to the woman who she was, and then the nurse took the same amount of time explaining who the woman was to her. They shook hands. To her surprise, she was just a friend. He was originally from Tucson, Arizona, and had no family in the area. He traveled the world and settled in Louisiana. He was thirty-seven years old. His friend Adriana was so informative, as if she believed she was privy to the information.

That uneasy feeling she first felt upon seeing her existed no longer. She explained that she was a businesswoman who owned her own press company. She shared the little secret that she was the woman responsible for the newspaper gossip column *411*. Adriana wasted no time asking her a million questions. Her first question was not what she expected. Instead of asking were the things she printed in the newspaper true, Adriana asked how she knew Marcus. Telling her Marcus was just the delivery guy was not working. She read straight through her. She tried to give the illusion that he was nothing more, but her heart sang a different tune and Adriana heard it. She wanted that man! She desired his smell on her skin. She dreamt of him often and used the thought of his flesh inside of her to satisfy her fantasies when self-pleasuring. His broad shoulders, wavy thick brown hair, and rippled chest made her call out to him when he was not close.

She found herself thinking about the heavy boxes he handled. Not once had she ever heard him complain about the weight of them or having to go to each office to pick them up when they should have been waiting by the front desk for him. Determined to get more information, she offered to take Adriana to dinner. She treated Adriana to the meal she had been craving before this unpleasant situation. They rode down the avenue in complete silence. Adriana almost had no idea of her reasoning. She couldn't quite clarify her reasoning to herself, so she didn't even try. She permitted the jazz to soothe the unspoken suffering they both were enduring. Adriana's friend and her secret lover! *My secret lover*, she thought. A lover she had never talked to, touched, rubbed, or caressed in the physical. According to her wet sheets, he was her man, a man who could be loved by her.

As they drove up to Red Lobster's curbside pickup, Adriana released a smug laugh. It was as if she was reading her private thoughts.

She turned to Adriana and asked, "What's so funny?"

She giggled this time. "You are her!"

"I am who?" she asked.

"You are the woman who he dares not to attempt. He wants you, wants you over dinner and a salad. He wants to take long walks with you and have nonsexual intimate conversation with you."

The information started flowing out of Adriana as if she knew what she needed to hear.

"You are beautiful. He described you down to the scratch on the side of your cheek. Your long locks of curls are just as he imagined they would be in his hands as he played through your hair."

Just then, a vibration came from within her purse. Startled, they both jumped. Chill bumps ran up her spine and tears filled her eyes. She could not move fast enough to get to the phone. Unknown caller! Instead of the call she hungered for, it was an international client lost on the time zone.

"Good morning," the gentleman said.

His broken English was driving her crazier than the fact that he was not who she wanted to talk to. Her unsettled nervousness enabled her to brush him off. She excused herself from the conversation, but only for a tap on the window to again distract her from the information being given like a gift. She accepted the food, paid the bill, and looked for Adriana to finish. As they approached a red light, the phone rang once more. She grabbed it this time. She tried to relieve her of the stress. She pushed the speakerphone and the nurse began to speak.

"Is this Marcus John's family?"

"Yes, this is."

"He is out of surgery. Dr. Jolinski would like to speak with Adriana."

"This is her," she said aloud.

"If it's possible, would you be able to come back to the hospital?" she said.

Without missing a beat, both women replied they would be there in three minutes.

Chapter 10
Fearful

Getting to the urgent care floor on the fourth floor was a journey. The halls seemed to go on forever. The doors doubled the more they walked. The elevator opened and closed six times for those going down and not once for the up arrow. So, they took the stairs. Running didn't seem to be that much of a chore in this case, especially since she was running for the love of her life. Well, she wanted him to be the love of her life. He *had* to be the love of her life.

He had spoken her full name before passing out. "Your name is Trina Monroe," was the last thing he mumbled. She found him. She thought, *He could be my heaven-sent.* With her arrival not being too late, she had saved his life. She desired for him to save her, for them to save each other.

Being thirty-three years old, she deserved a man who had the ability to love her through her weaknesses and strengths. She needed him to have the ability to permit her to stand tall and rest her feet when she felt weary. He could be that man. No children, never married, and the eldest of three siblings, life was his to devour. He had traveled the world and grew as a man from such determination. This was more information his high school friend had gifted to her.

Adriana was a beauty in her own right. The thirty-eight-year-old lesbian's words made her believe she would have Marcus for herself if he were a woman. That's how highly she spoke of him.

They tiptoed to his area. Butterflies consumed her stomach and tears filled her eyes. She cried. She cried tears of joy and fear. She cried for this man like a wife wept for a sick husband. He wasn't her spouse, but the love felt the same.

Adriana held her while she entwined her fingers with hers. They were a braided flesh. As they cruised to the curtain in urgent care, Dr. Jolinski moved it.

"He made it through surgery successfully," he informed them. "Unfortunately, we are uncertain of his recovery due to the amount of stab wounds he received. He lost a substantial amount of blood and had to have a blood transfusion. The transfusion went well. The rest is on him. He has to have a will to live through such a traumatic experience. The next twenty-four hours is for him to decide if life is what he wants." Dr. Jolinski then asked, "Does he have anything to fight for? Is there anyone he would enjoy hearing from?"

"We are all he has here," Adriana said.

"Well then, you both need to speak to him. Remind him what his life is, and why he should come home to you. The nurses are finishing the priming of his room. He was being prepped for a strong recovery."

As the doctor walked off with them toward the family waiting room, a loud buzzing sounded off. Without saying a word, the doctor turned and ran back to Marcus's room. Startled and confused, Adriana and her fell into each other, struggling to balance themselves. They were uncertain of their bond, but they knew they cared for the same soul in different ways. They ran to the curtain where the doctor stood in amazement.

Speechless, Marcus reached out for them. Then he reached up further for her hair. Despite his coughing fit, he wanted nothing more than to touch her. He was her love, and she was his lifeline. He gave them a second chance. He kissed Adriana. He loved her.

Marcus had been stabbed twelve times: three times in the back, twice in the shoulders, and once in the lung. The rest of the wounds were throughout his chest and legs. Whoever did this wanted him dead. The detectives, who stood closely by, had questions. They wanted to know if he saw anything, if he knew his attacker, if he had heard their voice. They questioned what the attacker wanted and if they had taken anything?

She became overwhelmed. She wanted to run from the madness, but her feet would not move from underneath her. It was as if her feet were planted in the cement of the hospital's floor. Marcus desired her comfort. He sensed her uneasy heart, even though they had not yet been properly introduced.

After Adriana and the doctor took control, dismissing everyone from the curtained area, Marcus pulled at her. His oxygen mask came off as he tugged her arm once, moving her closer to him. While rubbing her hair, he spoke. What he said was both unexpected yet exactly what she hoped to hear.

"My name is Marcus. Marry me?"

Two years, twenty-four hours, thirty-two minutes, and five seconds later as the sun set, she became Mrs. John. Standing on the white sandy beaches of Hawaii with the sun at their backs, they became one during a small, simple ceremony. Nothing was formal about their lives together, and neither was their wedding. His best man was a woman, while the bride's sister, Lolita, gave her away. Pure whiteness, their clothes, love and affection are how they started their union. Their love was as the sky above, clear and understanding.

Pureness, cleanliness was the actual act of lovemaking. The beginning of the union, she learned to respect the power of love. She searched for something deep within him. She looked into his eyes and found a soul. Nothing empty. He took her into his arms, into his mouth, as she begged him to never let her go. His beauty was something she could not dream of. He was more. He was a sensual sensation.

He started with her eyebrows, rubbing each hair. He kissed the space between the two. Moving his way down her face, he kissed the beginning of her nose. He started at the bone structure. Just as the curve began, so did he. She felt his manhood rise. The spirit of flesh wandered throughout her. He spoke gently into her ears. One at a time, he caressed her thoughts.

"Loving you is a joy that I shall enjoy for the rest of our lives."

Switching to her right ear, he repeated those same exact words. With every word, she went with him. She freed herself. Knocking down the walls she built around her heart, he spoke to her, singing a song of forever. She moved closer to him. There was no pressure for her to love him. He loved her. It was nothing other than ecstasy. There was no one around to distract the flow that moved through their sheets. It was a feeling of naturalness. She came with him. Freeing herself, she let go. She let go of Mr. Man. This was her man, her husband. She was he and he was she. He understood her. *Honeymoon!* She was silently scared, and just as she was ready to jump from him, he pulled her closer to him and whispered, "No, don't move. Baby, I have you. Mrs. John, you are safe."

He told her to close her eyes, but she refused.

"Close your eyes, Mrs. John."

Small teasing of her neck allowed her to give in. She closed her eyes, fearful that when she opened them, she would be alone. Still, she closed them.

He whispered, "Relax, you. You, Mrs. John, are not my friend. You are not afraid of me. You are my wife for life."

In the deep distance, she heard the cracking of the wind. She went with him. As he wanted her to do, she absorbed every word. The rain began tapping on the windowsills. His words pulled at her. He understood her. He knew she needed to learn to trust, to let go. He took his time with her.

During their first night together, the storm rolled in with the darkness of the clouds. His words were a slow jam to her heart. They began a melody with the beat of her soul. She took his hand, and he led her to the head of the bed. He put his arms around her and the melody sang louder. She heard drums. She saw the notes of the song he sang to her; they were whole notes. He wanted her to hear him; he wanted her to believe him. He danced. He was not going home to anyone else. He was hers to keep, to admire. He was hers. This night was all about her. This night was theirs.

Rubbing in between her thighs, he found the softest place on earth. He licked and passionately found his new home. This was her little secret. This secret was manacling. It held onto her, ringing life into her soul. Crutching on to his neck, she raised her hips to his lips. The wetness started to fall. The rain poured down on the universe, while her personal wetness showered her husband. She heard herself say it. *My husband.* He was her husband, and he followed the natural flow of their bodies.

At the top of heaven's gate, he screamed out. Going through the clouds, he rested. Tightening her limbs, she cried. She cried out for forgiveness. She bit into the skin of his arm; he pulled her closer. They grew. It grew. His manhood grew. Her moans deepened. His tongue deepened. The candles continued to burn. They were all that was on earth. His motions moved against her. He taught her; he learned her.

Just when she could take no more, he removed her legs and kissed her outer thigh while she rotated her body counterclockwise against the wall. She was standing upside down; he was turning her out. With her facing him, he devoured her vagina, and she tried to find what made him tick. Action took over her. His penis was down her throat, grinding her mouth. They began to find the angels' pathway to heaven. He laid her back down on the bed and in his arms. This time, he had them around her waist from behind. He entered her.

"Mrs. John…Mrs. John," he called out.

Unable to answer, she nodded. She nodded to let him know his entrance did not kill her. He was not her demise. He was new life, a new breath. He pulled out and reentered her, pulling her closer into him. Her hips rocked with him. Her pussy drummed a beat against his foreskin. Just the head accepted the rumbling she offered.

She continued with the beat he had started. She became untamed, an irrational brute. They made love, but now she wanted to fuck. She desired to change his mind. She was more than softness. She could fulfill his aggressive side. He had it all in one package, and that package was her. The harder she went, the more she heard her name. Arousal was the goal; that was succeeded. One extra roll of her hips, and that was it. She felt her husband for the first time. He ran down her leg. The heat between them was like a flame on flesh. They burned slow. Wanting…needing…desiring!

"Your hands told me secrets. They told me that you were more than mine," were her last words before falling into a deep slumber.

Allowing all the walls to fall from her heart, she fell asleep in his arms. They woke to the sun rising over their faces. With the clouds gone and the rain finished, there was an unexpected knock at the door, reminding them that they were not alone on earth.

Chapter 11
When Morning Comes

She called Mr. and Mrs. John awake, and she would not stop. Adriana continued to knock and call out for them like she had gone mad. Laughing, they opened the door and were greeted with the largest bouquet of flowers and fruits.

Sitting her gifts down only took a few seconds. Jumping in bed with them had become her normal routine. She moved to a comfortable position between her husband and his best friend. At first, this had been difficult. However, it became strangely easier as she began to view Adriana as her sister rather than Marcus's best friend.

Twenty minutes later, there was another knock on the door. With them being too lazy to get up, Adriana answered the pounding. Lolita ran in, and it soon turned into a mini sleepover. She climbed on the bed next to Marcus's feet, while he and his wife laughed. *What is a honeymoon without your best friends,* she thought.

They had already planned their afternoon prior to arriving. They were to take a local cruise and have dinner at the luau that would have a large roasted pig, dancers, music, and fire. Having always been intrigued with fire, she loved the intensity of the flames, which cracked, popped, and sizzled as midnight crept upon them.

2:00 a.m.

As they walked along the ocean, the moon reflected off the water. Skinny-dipping? Nah! Instead, they found a pitch-black cave. Honestly, she was eager to plant their love there. They didn't dare to sleep there. They just found an adventure in its place. These types of voyages led to an undertaking—sex.

Salty beads of sweat poured off them. He gave her the runaround. Her man loved her body to the end of the seashore. He was out to prove he was capable of gratifying her urges. He was just as spontaneous as her!

With only two days left for their honeymoon, they had yet to make it to the other side of the island or just stay in the bed all day. So, that was their plan for the next day. They would ignore the door knocks and screams. The curtains would stay closed and the blinds shut. They deserved this, and they would enjoy the time alone by having breakfast in bed, lunch in the shower, and dinner on the floor.

The next morning, there were no knocks, screaming, or pre-made plans. She would have worried about Adriana and Lolita's absence if it weren't for the fact that they were two adults sharing a room. Therefore, she knew they were fine. She and Marcus cradled in bed. Their breakfast consisted of devouring each other, nibbling on breasts and necks, licking whipped cream-covered toes, and eating apple slices and pineapple chunks from each other's belly. This feast was incredible. Lovemaking and food—the perfect combination. Marcus was attentive, assertive, and aggressive at the right times.

Half a day left. Their plane was scheduled to take off at two o'clock in the afternoon local time. Three days had not been enough. Dinner lay across the floor. Lobster tails, crab cakes, and crab legs for her. Her favorite! Marcus chose steak, potatoes, and string beans. A true American meal! The fireplace roared at them. If for nothing but the look of it, it made dinner that much better.

After eating, they cleaned up their mess, showered, and went to bed. She didn't feel well after the seafood and even had a fever. So, he rubbed her tummy and spoon-fed her some Pepto-Bismol. There's never a good time to get ill, but at least it happened on the last night of their honeymoon.

Throughout the night, she regurgitated several times. It was weird. They blamed it on the native seafood. She was embarrassed, while he loved her through it all. Every time she moved, he moved. Afraid it might be food poisoning; he wanted to take her to the hospital. Mrs. John, on the other hand, decided sleep was more important. With a twelve-hour flight back home ahead of her, she was truly intrigued to sleep, and that they did.

The next morning, the alarm sounded and there was pounding on the door. Lolita and Adriana were back. They were all packed, bags by the door, and tip on the desk. Their paradise was over, and they were faced with the reality of returning home. Three steps outside the doorway, and to her dismay, she regurgitated. Everyone stopped and looked at her, blown away that she was ill.

A cap-full of Pepto-Bismol and a bottle of water later, they were on the plane. Once in flight, she put her headphones on and went to sleep. Waking up, she realized she had been only napping for a few minutes. The urge to vomit was gone, but her head still throbbed. Adriana and Lolita looked over her as if she were a sick child. She wished they would look over the yelling child in the front row.

Back when she was a young adult, kids were not a high priority in her world. She just didn't have a lot of experience with them. There are no nephews or nieces in their immediate family. Now that she was older, she found a soft spot for them.

She walked to the front where the child and its parent were seating. The mother was in tears, unsure of what to do for her child. From the looks of it, he was overheated. His skin had a red tone to it, and little red bumps covered his neck. She offered to hold him while the mother went to the restroom. Her return was longer than she expected. So, she walked back to her seat with the little boy.

Not even a minute later, there was commotion in the back of the plane. She began to worry. It had been twenty-five minutes since the mother went to the restroom, and a line had formed near the door of the restroom. Someone proceeded to bellow. She started to feel perplexed about the situation. Marcus suggested she stay seated until things calmed down.

The stewardess came over the intercom and announced, "We have to regretfully inform you that we have to make an emergency landing. The restroom in the back is out-of-order. However, the two restrooms in the front and middle are in operation."

As the stewardess laid the phone down to speak with her coworker, she forgot to disconnect the call and the seated passengers ended up hearing parts of the conversation. *Body found...she is dead from what seems like an overdose. Maybe heroin...needle found!*

What the hell, she thought. She and Marcus stood immediately, anxiety consuming them. Afraid they had the dead woman's child, they rushed to inform the stewardess. Her illness was strong but not strong enough to slow her down. Lolita looked. Adriana woke up. Dragging her feet, she tried running. They were dismissed, warned to go sit down! So, they ended up back where they started…in their seats with a child who was not theirs.

She became emotional. Tears filled her eyes. Unlike herself, she was clueless as to what their next course of action would be. So, she just prayed. The seatbelt sign came on as they prepared to land. She shared her seatbelt with the boy, placing it across his body as she held him close to her. Thousands of feet below, they could see the flashing lights of fire trucks, ambulance, and police vehicles. Reporters were in position. They had a story, and it would be told.

After landing the plane safely, Angie, the stewardess, came back on the speaker and asked everyone to remain seated until further notice. Mrs. John insisted that she listen to her as she passed by, but she ignored her request. Detectives who gave directions rushed the plane. First class was let off first. Business class followed and then coach.

They were seated in the airport. She still had this child and had no idea what to do with him. Due to the reckless acts of the individual on the plane, who was now dead, she found herself responsible for a toddler. Faced with no other choice, she proceeded to the ticket counter so she could turn the child over to the authorities. While walking, Marcus called out to her. When she turned around it was as if God had answered her silent prayer. The lady was not dead after all. She was not an addict. She loved her son and was coming to get him.

Once his mother reached where they stood, she began explaining what happened. She had gone to use the restroom, but both were occupied. So, she decided to use the restroom in the coach area. When she tried to return to where they were seated, the commotion started and everyone was ordered to stay where they were. His mother expressed her thanks for them taking care of her son. As she handed over the child, she wished her a good life.

Hours later, they boarded a different plane and were back in the air. Her nerves were better and her headache gone. Looking back at Lolita and Adriana, they were sound asleep. Marcus was knocked out, as well. She listened to her music and watched the movie until she fell asleep again. This time, she awakened to them landing. They were home for the first time as a married couple. They grabbed their luggage and rushed to their humble abode.

Chapter 12
Home Sweet Home

6:00 a.m.

The chance of it happening when she got home was nothing short of a surprise. She vomited as soon as they touched the front porch. That was it. Marcus refused to listen to anything else she had to say. He put the luggage in the house, snatched the keys off the wall, and off to the hospital they went.

They traveled down I-90 toward St. Allegis Hospital. Reaching the emergency room, they decided urgent care would be better. Stomach flu was her personal diagnosis. They checked in at the register desk, provided the insurance card, and waited. Once they called for her, Marcus accompanied her to the examination room, where she was instructed to undress and give a urine sample. This was not her idea of a homecoming. She honored her husband's first wishes, though. They asked the routine questions. *Is there a chance you could be pregnant? Are you allergic to anything? What have you eaten recently?* So on and so on. The questions didn't stop until the results of her urine sample came back. Dr. Do Nothing came in and said they had the answer to her flu-like symptoms.

While looking down at the results, he announced, "You're pregnant."

"We are pregnant."

"We're pregnant."

"What, we're parents?"

"We are parents."

Shocked by this news, she and Marcus repeated this back and forth. They were lost in words and space. She was upset, while Marcus was ecstatic about the fact that he would soon be a father.

After she got dressed, they left the hospital and went to White

Castle. Her phone rang, and Lolita's name appeared on the screen. She answered.

"Can we meet? I need to talk to you." Lolita's tone was serious.

Before she could reply, Marcus's phone chimed and Adriana's name appeared. She also wanted to meet.

They became concerned. He looked at her as if she had the answers, but she had none. They made it to their house at the same time Adriana and Lolita did. They pulled into the driveway. One by one, they got out of their cars. They were weird, and she was starving.

After they were all seated in the living room, she started stuffing herself with the small, greasy soy burgers and side order of fries. She chewed; they mumbled. She couldn't understand a thing they were saying over her own thoughts of being pregnant.

Marcus pinched her arm. "Are you listening to them? Did you hear what they said?"

"No, babe, I'm lost in thought," she whispered.

"Well, babe, you need to listen."

"I hope you are not disappointed," Lolita said.

Adriana sighed. Marcus smiled, but she had no idea what was going on. For her, she repeated herself.

"I'm leaving the country."

Silence fell over the room. It became so quiet that she believed she heard the birds chirping and the snails sliding through the grass. In her mind, she could even hear the wings on the flies flying in the neighbor's house. It was too quiet. Lolita's mussed look on her face was dramatic. Adriana's suppressed feelings were more than she could deal with. She deserved answers. Marcus's ridiculous understanding of life was not helping her. She loved them both no matter what, but this? When? How? Why? Why now? The questions started to fill the room, and when they could not take any more, they hushed her. They dared to tell her to shut up in her home. She hushed just for the purpose of hearing what they had to say.

Adriana burst into tears. She cried and laughed until Mrs. John started laughing with her. She was unsure of what they were laughing about, but she laughed. Marcus laughed. Lolita cried and laughed. The house was no longer a disdain. Life resumed its place.

When she attempted to stand up, things shut down again. Marcus stood with her. He caught her to help balance from the anger that roared in her. Not because of what she could have been upset about, but more so because she was unsure of everything coming at her. First, she got ill on the last day of her honeymoon. Second, there was a death on the plane ride home. Third, she found herself caring for what she thought was a motherless child. Fourth, she found out she was pregnant, and now, she learned that Lolita and Adriana were leaving the country.

Trying to storm off, she lost her balance and pulled Marcus down with her. Concerned for the baby and her, he stopped laughing. He could not take any more. He demanded for them to speak up, but she spoke first. She couldn't take any more tonight, either. If they had more news that would kill her before she made it to the restroom, she demanded that they save it until the next day.

Lolita molded her face with her right hand, kissed her cheek, and looked deep into her eyes. She began begging her to understand, to love her as she loved her.

Then, while kneeling on the floor, she opened her mouth and said, "Joke's on you."

The laughter roared through the house. It hid in the open spaces. It seeped under the front door. The laughter took chances of coming back and getting louder in her face. They laughed hard and together.

Joke's on me! What in the hell are they talking about?

Marcus left her on the floor as they began to stand in unison, backing away from the area they once were sitting in. They picked up their pace as her balance was found. She stood strong and chased them through the house.

"Baby, stop running! You might fall again," Marcus screamed.

"Stop running and I'll stop chasing you," was her response.

Folding himself in the corner of the bathroom next to the shower, he threw his hands in the air, as if he waving a white sheet and begging for forgiveness.

"It was a setup. When we found out you were pregnant, I called them. Realizing you would strangle me with your bare hands for telling them before you had a chance to, I set this up so they could tell you what I did."

He was now pleading for his life. Making their way back to the sitting area, they had flooded the room with gifts. Boy and girl stuff; teddy bears and stuffed animals in pink and blue. Their child didn't even have a room yet and had more stuff than she could look at. She disliked them a lot, while loving them to death. Their joke was well planned out. It was in its own right magnificent. Tears rolled down her face at the same time the hugs came. Their house was more than a shelter. It was an open space filled with love. It was their home.

They were home.

Home sweet home.

Time passed quickly as they laughed, cried, and talked about politics. They were blessed to have witnessed something most of them thought they would never see, an African American president. One hundred days into his presidency, he was concerned with the deaths of many armed services men and women, the budget, homeless persons, and the unemployment rate. She was simply concerned with their unborn child. There was a side conversation going on, and it was then she found herself thinking about her childhood. Back then, it was the small things that drove her crazy. However, as a mother-to-be, she could see how those things made her the woman that she was. Her mother often spoke in quotes. One of her favorite quotes that she would recite before she went to school went like this:

Do more than exist—live.
Do more than touch—feel.
Do more than look—observe.
Do more than hear—listen.
Do more than listen—understand.
Do more than talk—say something!
—*Henry Rhoades*

She must admit her mother's recital of this quote worked her nerves. At times, she wanted to scream, *I got it, Mom! I got it!* Today, she says that quote every morning after her morning prayer. She thanked God for waking her with working limbs and a peace of mind. *What can I teach this creature growing within me?* I thought.

Her name was called, disrupting her daydreaming. Her dear husband wanted to know that she was okay. She just looked and replied, "Of course." She did not want to share her fears. She did not want him to worry about her too much more than what he had already been doing.

Lolita and Adriana departed before she had a chance to tell them that she wanted to go out and eat. Marcus decided they should stay in and get some rest. He would cook, and she would actually realize he had an uneasy feeling from her running and falling. She did as he asked; she lay on the couch and watched television.

A few hours passed, and Marcus woke her up to eat. She hadn't even noticed she fell asleep while watching *Matlock*, a classic show. The aroma of garlic filled her nasal passages. He held a plate filled with chicken Kiev, buttered broccoli, and garlic butter rice. He also made his famous French garlic bread covered with chunks of garlic and shredded marble jack cheese. She was in food heaven. It couldn't get any better.

Chapter 13
Julius Santana

Fear rose within me and seemed to carry me to a far-off land. It consumed my strength with each breath I inhaled. I wanted to free myself from such despair. I closed my eyes, giving into the pressure of freedom. I was at a loss...my comfort, that is. I tossed and turned. I wanted to believe it was my couch causing my discomfort. The pain I carried in my lower back was surreal, strong enough to control a horse. Yet, my mental ability would not give in to its power. My body wanted rest while my spirit needed to savage all its strength for the day ahead. I was trapped in a state of confusion. Was I sleeping or awake? I needed answers, but my body was too heavy to rise.

I heard the yelling of two unknown voices: one male and one female. They were angry, upset at one another. Their voices became closer to the space I tried to hide in. The sound of the ocean surrounded me, the drumming beat of each wave protecting my ears, drowning them out. I heard kicking and banging as if someone was coming through the walls and doors all at once. I felt that creature over me.

More sounds, more voices. This time they were familiar. I wanted to feel safe, but I wasn't. There was an abundance of creatures, spirits, and objects around me, yet no one to protect me. I gave one last try to save myself from such fear. I placed my feet on the floor beneath me. That's when I knew something was wrong. I was not myself. I was in my body; however, my soul was off, like a half-in, half-out type of feeling. I considered a thin cloud of hopefulness strong enough to hold up my weight. My feet dragged across the floor. My arms were too heavy to carry the idea of holding on to a wall.

With one arm across my chest, I looked into the bathroom mirror, and to my surprise, it was me. I was sick; something had happened to me while I was asleep. My mouth was twisted to one side, while my tongue dangled below my chin. Fear rose within me again, this time strong enough to push me over. Instead of falling on my side, I was caught by something I was hiding from. My body tensed with every word that slithered out of his mouth.

"Don't fight it and go to it," he said with a tone that smelled of the best revenge. He snickered. "Good riddance, bitch."

Letting go of my shoulders, he disappeared into the kitchen, leaving me in a daze of confusion, fear, and pain. Sad moments my life was covered in. I could hear my life going on without me. My children talked and laughed with the man who was killing me. They were not safe. I did not keep them safe. The devil was here in the flesh, and my body and mind were consumed with death. He was winning, and I was left to wake up.

I awakened to quietness. There was no one fighting outside my door. There was no running water and no one beating on the door. I was lying in my bed alone. The fan to my left was on medium speed, and the television was off. I picked up the phone and dialed; I needed to know was I asleep or awake. The dream lay on top of my skin, under my red satin blanket with me. When I moved, it moved. This dream was no dream; it was a nightmare. I had been resting all of thirty minutes, and my life was completely shaken up in that short amount of time.

Three days later, I was okay with not sleeping. The backs of my eyelids were too dark. I feared he might be there waiting for me again. His plan may have included my demise in the depths of a peaceful slumber. The strength of his evilness reached me in my awakened life. I looked for him around corners. While standing in the shower, I expected to see him when I pulled back the shower curtain. When walking out to my car, would he be there sitting on its hood? His ability to haunt me taunted me. It was important his demise come before my own. Him six feet under would be the only way I knew he couldn't harm me. Extreme measures were the way to go.

Three days later, I was standing in the police station. Looking back, I wonder what they would have said if I expressed my concerns, my fears, my exhaustion from the lack of sleep because his devilishness made me paranoid. Instead, I kept it to myself. I hid the *real reason why I was filling out an application for a gun permit and signing up for the class that would give me the right to conceal my weapon wherever I want. My life or his death! It couldn't be me. I had responsibilities. My life was planned for my children and me. We could not fail. We were to succeed, leaving poverty where it wanted us to live for eternity behind. I was born to live a life of stressful basic struggles.*

What would we eat? We surpassed those issues. My issues today were more than that. I no longer worried about shoes and clothes. My fears were eating me alive, and not until I did away with his body, his evil ways, would I have a peaceful rest. Unfortunately, I rest here in prison. They, the court system, did not understand that was the only way. They had failed so many men and women from their abuser. I could not be a part of a system that failed. I needed to succeed. His death was my success; he is no longer harming others. He is not able to corner me in my bedroom, yelling in my face. He can no longer hold my face until the skin is a mere disguise for my bone, hurting. He no longer chips away at my soul, picking and pulling at my hair, slapping me during sex in the name of love. I am no longer the blame for his mishaps, addictions, and failures. I'm free to sleep with my back to the door, not worrying if he will kick the door in. I no longer concern myself with seeing him sitting in my car with my demise on his thoughts. I am no longer.

I leave this letter to say goodbye. Today, my fears are my children hating me for taking our life and turning it upside down in search of love, for not protecting them through protecting myself. I was a failure, and for that, I am giving my final notice and prayers to my Heavenly Father, loving all those who just did not see the pain I carried within.

That's how her Monday morning started on March 7, 2008. She wanted to die. She had killed a man, and she believed her life was over. She called her lawyer and cried while explaining what happened. He was confused with what she was saying. He asked if she wanted him to come over. She told him yes and that she was ready to turn herself in. Her children were off to school, and they would have to go to her sister's home was what she told him.

Her body ached from the struggle from the night before. He chased her through the house and threw her against the marble casing of their fireplace. Her fingers were numb. Her cheeks were bruised from sleeping on the carpet where he forced her to lay after kicking her in the back.

It amazed her why she chose this man of all men that would have loved to marry her. She said the words "I do" in the outskirts of the Florida Keys. The sand was soft; the water smashed against the rocks, and her lace dress flowed with the help of the gentle breeze blowing. He wore a white button-up Sean John shirt, and his white slacks perfectly hung from his body, hugging his ass so nicely. She was in heaven. As night fell, the sky filled with beautiful shades of purples, pinks, and baby blues. They danced underneath the stars and made love on the sand in front of the exclusive hotel. The way his lips caressed her neck made her want him to go lower. He covered her stomach with his hands and rubbed her. She moaned from the pleasurable sensation. Goose bumps protruded from every pore of her body. The more she wanted it, the more he touched her. She wanted to make love to him, her husband. Her hair fell out of its bun, and her pink-trimmed lily flower landed in between her legs.

Mr. Santana teased her with her favorite flower. He slid the flower in her mouth and had her bite down on the stem so no one could hear her moans. Just as she did as he instructed, his tongue rolled over the lips of her pussy. As he requested, she had shaved the day before, so she was able to feel each stroke of his tongue. The wetness flowed from her. The wetness of his mouth made her delirious. He teased her to no end, his dick creeping inside her walls to untouched areas. Before she could get a word out, he dug deeper. His back moved like a snake on a hunt for its prey. Her legs wrapped around his neck. He controlled her; at that very moment, he owned her. He owned the idea of controlling her body, allowing her to succumb to her sanity. The sand surrounded the area they rolled in. The water slammed against the bottom of their feet. The stars and moon above them disappeared. That was their first date as husband and wife, Mr. and Mrs. Santana.

A knock on the door pulled her from her daydream. Her lawyer was knocking. Time to answer her call to jail! Arthur entered and seemed more confused now than when he had spoken with her on the phone. Again, she explained herself. He sat her down and asked if she was sure of what had happened. He needed to know if she had taken anything before going to bed. She told him that she took a couple sleeping pills her husband, who was a psychiatrist, had given her a few weeks after her accident. Her husband had become a new man over the past ten years, not the great man that she once knew. As she reminisced about the not-so-good changes in her husband, Arthur pulled her from her thoughts, speaking to her in a manner that did not make any sense to her.

"I believe you had a nightmare," was the first thing he said. "Your husband is not dead. He's in the office getting his case files prepared for the court appearance he has this morning. So, why you assume you killed him frightens me."

Imagine the look on her face when she realized she wasn't free, that he would be back to corner her and fault her for his failures. She would be beaten on the floor of their living room. The dinner she prepared would be smashed into the floor and thrown across the walls of their dining area. She would end up scrubbing the walls until her knuckles were white, while waiting for him to fall asleep. The silence in the house would drive her crazy. He hated the fact that she hadn't given him a child. She knew if he had a son, he would only teach him to beat another woman, and she would not birth him a daughter that would follow in her footsteps and fall weak to the opposite sex. She refused to be a part of such disaster. So, he hated her, and the more he failed at having his own children, the more she became bruised from the one person who was supposed to protect her. Despite her punishment, she continued to take her birth control and endure the beatings.

Her lawyer thought it would be a good idea if she went to the in-patient hospital to be tested for PTSD, post-traumatic stress disorder. She had heard of it, but she didn't trust him, and especially since he worked for her husband. Instead of going along with what he suggested, she told him that she would rather go to her brother's home for a while. It was out in the country; no one would be around to stress her the hell out or beat her for that matter.

So, she left. It was her way out. Leaving helped her regain her hope. She even saw herself having children in her future.

After being gone for two weeks and with no pills in her system, she went back. She eventually stopped taking the birth control pill, and less than a month later, she was pregnant. However, that didn't stop him from physically abusing her. He wanted to protect their unborn child, so her face became his punching bag instead of her stomach. Her nature glow was not so natural; make-up covered the scars.

Three kids and fifty extra pounds later, she left her husband. She tried to remember why she came back. When she remembered, she began to cry. That fucking lawyer had tricked her. He had called her, convincing her that she could not make it without any support from her dear husband. He convinced her to come back, stating her husband needed her. Looking back, she saw it was only about the money. With no prenuptial agreement, she owned him. She had him where he did not want to be. Her position gave her power, and she planned to use it immediately.

When she began packing, a sense of strength came over her. She was taking back her life. Too tired and with bags too large to run, she walked away. Not a speed walk, not even a creep. She strolled out of the front door as if she was going to the grocery store. She pulled one piece of luggage with one arm and carried another. She instructed the movers to lift, not drag the furniture. Her children were staying at her brother's ranch, where they were riding horses with no concerns of their new home. They would have a vacation in a strange new place. They would dip their toes in Lake Superior. Fresh fruit would be brought to their suite every morning. The pool would sparkle as the light from the sun hit it, and they would no longer hear the sound of thunder when there was no rain. They would enjoy themselves in the Land of Ten Thousand Lakes.

They were three nights into their trip, when the words came to her from His hands. Her hidden treasure had come to life in the middle of the night. Her children were sleeping, and she was typing on her laptop. The words flowed from her with no doubt of their meaning. She was given the power to take back her life. Now she had the strength and ability to strive for more than she had become. She typed in her private journal on her personal computer. Two pages later, she cried. She read it again and again. They were her words and she was proud of them.

Chapter 14
Take Back

In my short life, I have met a few wonderful people
There were people stuck in a situation they believed they were not able to overcome
They allowed their life to become a motionless photograph
With the negative thoughts they allowed within their ream of understanding
So, tonight, I give you the ability to take back what is rightfully yours
I give you back your power
The same power you forgot you had stored within yourself
I give it back to you
I speak for the blind and unheard
I am speaking to the strong and the weak
The rich and the poor, the lost and the found, I am speaking to you
I am speaking to everyone who has the power to read or hear someone tell you this
When they are trying to stop your pursuit of happiness
When they believe they have you trapped with nowhere to go
Speak with actions, no longer words that they refuse to hear
Speak with your heart of all hearts
You the weak and the fallen, take back your believeth in God
That you will have your way every morning you awaken
Take the church from those who preach the word of themselves instead of the word of God
You have the ability to live as long as you may with the power you were blessed with at birth
Take back the power to love whole and to be loved whole

You have the right to be successful
You have the ability to empower yourself
Wait on no one, because no one is waiting on you
You believe love ends with the closing of one door
Just as one door closes another shall open
You ask who am I to give you back your power
I AM a woman who has struggled with homelessness and the birth of fatherless children
I AM a woman who struggles as you do every morning when I awaken
I AM a woman who believes LOVE overpowers anything or anyone that crosses your path with harm on their heart for you
I AM a woman who believes the power we need every day is the same power we are blessed with when we open our eyes every morning to the sun, fog, snow or rain
I AM a woman who chooses to love whole and give without thought
I AM a woman who believes God has chosen all of us for a reason
Take back your power to raise your family in this technology-driven world
The family starts at home, not in the school or courthouse where your faith in God is not recognized
Not in a prison cell with bars holding you back from your reality
Bars are a state of the mind
There are individuals out in the world walking and breathing fresh air as if they, too, are behind bars
I say take back your life before life is taken from you!

    She felt like she was talking to a crowd. Then her emotions took over, like a man going to church for the first time. She was preaching to herself. This was meant for her, also. She would share this with every woman, man, and child she could reach. She wanted…no, she needed a support group. They all needed a support group. This had become Jojoba Essence, the nut to her salvation. Her support group would bring her closer to a better understanding.

    Going to their new home, she was determined to find a group that would benefit all of her needs. She would engage in adult conversations where someone would correct her when she was wrong, laugh when she wanted to cry, and just protect her.

Chapter 15
The Meeting

"I want to welcome you all to the lovely Jojoba Essence Journey. I appreciate each of your stories, sharing and giving a part of yourself to strangers such as us. I'm going to tell my story shortly, but first, I would like for you all to decide on a new name for yourself. This name will only be shared with the members of this journey. As I walk around, I will tap each of you on the shoulder. I will then give you a few moments to think of a seductive, role-playing name. I ask that you keep your blindfolds on until everyone has finished. Person one, what is your chosen name?"

"Punani Princess," she responded.

"Person two, what is your chosen name?"

Her response was, "A–Fact."

"How do you spell that?" she asked her.

"Capital A, dash, capital F, lowercase A–C–T."

She was intrigued, wondering exactly how she came about such a name. So, she asked, "What does it mean?"

"Anal fascination."

Very clever, she thought.

"Person three, what is your chosen name?"

Her response was different for sure. "Fate's Embrace," she said.

Again, she was impressed and curious as to why she chose such a strong statement for a name. Before she could ask, she shared her thoughts after taking a deep breath of fresh air.

"I am Fate's Embrace. I embrace my fate with a smile," she explained.

They laughed with her. She was right; that name would do her justice for the life of this journey.

Salina moved around the circle, touching the next person on the shoulder. "Person four, what is your chosen name?"

She astonished the group as a whole. She said it as if she was reading out of a dictionary.

Miss Thing replied, "Foment, which means to excite, stir up, whip up, encourage, urge, or fan the flames of."

That didn't sound seductive until she heard the meaning. She wanted her to add something, something that did not require her to say the definition for someone to get the full meaning. She seemed a little discouraged since she was the first of the group whose fictitious name Salina was not truly impressed with. After several drawn-out minutes, she settled on Elicit, giving the same feeling without the explained meaning. She agreed.

"Person five, what is your chosen name?"

She gave her a run for her money when she said, "Southern Feel, always warm."

They all giggled.

It was now her turn to share a part of herself. At the start of the meeting, she wanted to hear from the group first before sharing a part of herself. She knew her stories that led her to form such a support group, but she wanted to learn a part of them, for them to become familiar with each other.

The first meeting was held in the basement of a convention center, a room hidden from the rest of the world. They had come from every corner of the world to meet that night. As their planes landed, she had a small car waiting to pick up each one of them. They were to get inside the Ford Focus and put on a blindfold. They had to stay blindfolded until they were advised to remove them.

If the members were to decide they did not want to be a part of the group, they would have to make that decision while the blindfolds were still on. No one was to know one another until the contracts were signed and sealed in the vault that sat in the corner. These ladies were mothers, friends, and wives of prominent men throughout the country, as well as being prominent themselves. Their privacy was important!

After each lady signed the contracts that had been drawn up before they arrived, she began her story.

Chapter 16
Death Before Dishonor

Salina thought all men and women should have such sexual freedom. She didn't want to produce another swingers club; she wanted to produce fantasies in paradise. Paradise in alleys where anyone could see! Not to exclude oceans, lakes, cabins…hell, they could try for the solar system. Some craved heroin, crack, alcohol, meth, and shopping. Salina craved the first nut her husband gave her as a newfound freak.

Salina and her husband purchased abandoned buildings and fields of land that went on forever. They recreated the first Garden of Eve. Whatever could be thought of, they owned it across the nation. This team they decided to join took them as far as the United Kingdom and as close as their childhood park. They took pictures with no faces. They ordered their sexual fantasies, and Jojoba Essence provided the environment for it to happen.

Salina asked the members to understand that the journey they would embark on was their choice. With that, she instructed them to stand and repeat after her.

The sound of the chairs sliding back on the floor as five women stabilized their grounding echoed off the walls. With their right arm extended in front of them, they sounded off like the Navy's twenty-one gunshots for a fallen solider.

"Say these words with conviction! Repeat after me," Salina told them. "I embark on this journey with clarity, truth, and understanding. This evening, together we will bring forth life and rebirth to an opportunity we allowed to wither away. Death before dishonor; no divorce shall allow the disseverment of our union nor blood ties that are formed this evening."

As they recited the last statement of the pledge, a one-karat platinum diamond tennis bracelet was placed on the mwrist of each of the five women who chose to remain. Each bracelet had been engraved with the same wording: Death Before Dishonor.

They removed their blindfolds and discovered they were in the company of beautiful women who all had their own unique look. The members were from New England…Edinburgh to be exact…Jamaica, Puerto Rico, Brazil, and America, each having found a new home with this journey.

Words and smiles flooded the room. Fears erupted like a volcano. Salina walked around the circle embracing each the same as the one before. They were the Ladies of Jojoba Essence.

The Journey Begins
"Tonight is our night," said Salina.

They all had a turn to be head bitch. With that position, came the responsibility of the expedition and adventure. That included what they did, whom they did, and where it happened. Their rule of caution: *If you lie down with dogs, you'll awaken with fleas.*

Excellence was in order for proper performance. Being this was not Salina's first time, she decided she would conduct their first outing. Plain with controlled sexy! Each one wore a black and white t-shirt with the words "WE RUN THIS BITCH" printed on the front, while the back was left empty. Their bracelets glistened in the dimmest of lights; the clarity in their stones was beautiful. They rocked the pewter metallic Nappa Jessica Bennett Jilt's high heels; the straps crossed over and buckled in five places on the other side of their feet. They were open-toed, so their pedicures were easily seen. This was their signature look for the evening.

Dressing and meeting in the convention center, she wondered if New Jersey was ready for what they had to offer. When they arrived, they walked through the doors and stopped the show. Newark was not ready for them. With each of them in a flying geese stance, they got the attention of everyone in the room. Everyone immediately turned their heads, each for their own reasons: the ladies envied their shoes and jewelry; the men's eyes confessed they were happy to see new pussy. Their eyes screamed, *About damn time!*

While pouring their beauty in the room, they sashayed through the crowd, causing stress between couples. The ladies were not concerned by any of the drama building up. Tonight was a welcoming party for the ladies of Jojoba Essence. No fucking was allowed. This night they learned code words and met their sisters. They sat and discussed their new language. Every real team had their own way of conversing and communicating. Theirs would be in the language of "TWI", a language spoken by seven million people and found mainly in Ghana. This was going to be a task not easily conquered, but it would be mastered. The idea was to start off with small words and sayings before fully using the language in meetings and encounters with one another.

They were the center of attention while dancing and drinking together. No sequence applied to what they did; they just did it sexy and seductive. They took over VIP when they wanted to rest. Drinking an inexorable drink, their sexiness filled the club. It became an aroma no one could ignore. The dance floor became a fishbowl. They no longer wanted the attention; they were now in a position to play out their first mission. *Rule one: follow all rules of the night. You are not to touch anyone; no physical action. Rule two: bring your best story. Provide sets of words in story form that will allow every woman to see a vivid Kodak picture.*

While everyone prepared themselves, Salina ordered another round of Grey Goose, a smooth vodka that allows the truth to come from the mouth and the pussy of most women. When she returned with the waitress and the drinks, the ladies were ready and pulling straws to see who would go first.

The night was just beginning. A–Fact went first. She described the elicit gentleman across the room. He wore a black and gold ATL baseball cap, with a pair of baggy jeans that allowed the rim of his boxers to show. They gave the illusion that he was a "man of the streets". Long, hanging chains draped over his neck and down to the tip of his navel. He wore a fresh-pressed button-down. He was a true elite gentleman.

A–Fact told her story as if they had made love together. She set the scene in the basement of a gym. The basement was filled with a locker room for men and women alike. She walked down the stairs with fear in her heart. The only light available was the candles that led the way to the moment of his dreams. The water from the showers fogged up the windows and formed droplets of steam on the bricks of the walls. The timing was more than desirable; it was perfect.

Carl stood six-five and was completely naked, prepared to give a beating of a lifetime. He had just won a game and was ready to celebrate. The tone of the locker room was a sexy scene. He knew what he wanted, and she had all he needed for the night. As she walked toward him, she began removing her clothing. She pulled her supportive jersey over her head, leaving her 38-C lacy red bra exposed. She held his attention with the ability to remove her straight-leg jeans over her three-inch pumps. She called him to her as she bent down on her knees. She kissed the head of his penis and moaned as she engulfed his dick. She tasted all nine and a half inches as she kissed behind the drums of his penis. The citrus fruit seeped out of his pores, and she tasted all of it. In fact, she tasted all of him. She bit the inside of his thighs. She licked on the small of his back as she stood. After whispering in his ear how proud she was of him, she slithered back to her knees. Spreading her legs, she was able to insert her silver and pink double-header. She took two breaths, removed her hands from his penis, and began to kiss it again. She French-kissed his drums as if they could kiss her back. She dribbled them in her mouth against the tip of her tongue. She allowed them to slip out and then sucked all the strength in front of them.

His dick tastes so good, she thought.

She smiled as she told the story, giving the false impression she would do it again. The women were sitting on the edge of their seats waiting, damn near begging for more. Giving proper knowledge on how to suck the manhood of a man, she continued with her story. She explained how after a few more dips of going down his shaft, she was able to release him and allowed him to get his footing. He found his balance by sitting on the bench. She described how she rested her right foot on the bench next to him. She moved in closer and he spread her pussy lips apart. He wrapped her legs around his neck and lifted her off the ground. He stood and balanced her on the wall while keeping her in his mouth. Holding on to the back of his head she asked, *"How did you get here?"* Entering her pussy with his tongue, she cried for salvation, and begged him not to stop. The words came from deep within. Her body was captured by a man in a fantasy that only he could fulfill. Releasing her tasty juices, she came in his mouth. She dared to reach down to taste herself off his tongue.

Soaking themselves in the showers, the water covered them from head to toe. Taking her by her waist, he turned her upside down. Traveling the world had left him with an exotic taste for good yoni. She teased him with her tongue. Giving weight to the position, she rolled her head over his honey love. It was fresh, clean, and the evening carried on for hours. He came in her mouth over the cushions of her tongue and tonsils. Swallowing was joyous. His dick had a charisma that had the ability to call her back to him, and each time he called, she answered. Sliding her down out of his mouth, he penetrated her bewildering cloud. He stumbled into her silky soft walls. Finding a rhythm with the beat of the water, they climaxed together. She held her muscles around the neck of his manhood until he begged to be released. As the steam finally rose around them, the heightened awareness became obvious between the two of them; they were never alone.

The ladies were speechless with their mouths left open. Their glasses had been sat down on the table, and their backs were against the couches. They wanted to dance; they needed a chance to recoup. Giving them their space, they fixed their clothing and headed down the stairs. Absorbed by their own world, they did not realize a fight had broken out, and everyone was being ushered out of the club. The stories ended there. It was now 2:00 a.m., and they were exhausted. This evening had become a "to-be-continued" moment. They retired to their rooms and slept.

Chapter 17
Indicted

MIMS, Mother in Me Sisterhood, was more than it said it would be. It offered help to build capacity for self-support; it connected homeless young adults with living wage jobs, educational opportunities, job training, and basic employment for those who had never held a job. They enhanced their "financial literacy". The program itself was more than any youth with no family or skills could ask for. They gave them a beautiful place to live with their children, if they had any, and provided three meals a day. The only thing they had to do was take advantage of the opportunities MIMS offered. The social workers would come and meet each of the young ladies personally. Not only did they want their opinions on how the program was working, the social workers were even open to whatever ideas the young women had to make the program better for the next group of women entering into the program.

In the beginning, it was difficult getting used to the rules and regulations. They had curfews, contracts, bank accounts, and more. Every day was a new beginning, and they were taught to treat it as such. The online staff came in, checked their rooms, and spoke with the five graduates that were leaving in the next few weeks. The conversations started off with the question, *What are your goals once you leave here?* That question was followed by a list of questions about the different types of support they would need, or what they thought the agency could do to support them once they left. Only two of the five leaving had families that were actively positive role models. The social workers wanted them to understand the open-door policy; it was always open, but it was not a revolving door. Shockingly enough, their point was made: *Stay focused on your goals and success is merely a step away.*

Somehow, July 15, 2009 was different.

One of the girls seemed upset, confused, and hurt. Nicole cried most of the day and denied anything was wrong. The best Meka could do was offer her a shoulder to cry on. Nicole finally let the truth shine through at seven o'clock that evening after her daughter went to bed. Sitting on the windowsill in her room, she explained how it was not supposed to go that far, how it was a mistake. She wanted to take it back but didn't know how. She cried more before Meka had a clear understanding of what she was talking about. Her tears rushed out of her. She was emotionally unstable and Meka was convinced she should go for help, but Nicole wouldn't let her. The story took a strange turn when Meka decided to walk to Nicole and wrap her arms around her.

"Don't touch me," Nicole yelled at the top of her lungs. She crawled to a corner in her room and started rocking back and forth. While rocking, Nicole mumbled, "I didn't mean it, I didn't mean it."

Meka was speechless; she was genuinely concerned for Nicole's safety and feared for her physical health. Yet, Meka stepped back and listened. She wanted her to be able to express herself without her thoughts in the way. Lying across her bed, the words began to flow from her. It was as if a negative spirit was lingering around her, holding her back from her true self. Her words '*It was not supposed to happen*' were illustrated with the truth. It did happen, and it happened more than once. Nicole was homeless at one time and had no place to go; there was no family or friends to speak of. Unfortunately for her, she did what most young men and women did to survive a night on the streets. She slept with men and women for money, food, or a place to sleep.

The story was graphic and realistic. She described how these people who were looking out for her "best interest" would force her to have sex in front of cameras and with other people. She was tied up, beaten, put in cages, and made to lie about who she was and where she came from. She was involved in a sex trade that was happening right in her hometown of Minneapolis. Getting out seemed hopeless until one day, she found out she was pregnant. The woman, whom she had been living with, forced her to go get an abortion. The abortion took place in Duluth, MN, and that was the beginning of the end of the harsh reality of the only life she'd known. Nicole was able to escape from her sight by wandering the hallways after the procedure was completed. The woman that she knew as her pimp was searching for her as she hid in the garbage can in the alley. The day was an unfair ending to a life in hell. Her freedom was hers to claim. Yet, she was lost. With nowhere to go again, she slept under the Bong Bridge with the adult rainbow family. After one week of that lifestyle, someone put her in contact with a gentleman who was able to sign her up for a housing program for homeless youth. But before she went through the program, she lived with him for a few months. While living with him, she became pregnant again. This time, she kept the little girl. Her daughter, Faithful!

Today was a graceful step into her future, and then the mail was delivered. Nicole received documents from the court system that said Fred was asking for full custody of their daughter whom he had never met. His reasoning was that she was not capable of taking care of a child without the support or stability of the structure she was leaving. *She was being indicted for her past!* A past she had no control over, a past she left behind three years ago.

The room began to close in on her. She was losing the battle with herself. She was not focused on the future or her goals. Her past was knocking on her door and she was about to answer it without asking who it was. Danger was near. She was stuck in time, a time she had no control, no voice, and she doubted the young responsible woman she had become. Meka suggested she read her poems and find a support group, one that could support her in her time of need. A group of outsiders who would not judge her and who could see the whole picture with honesty. They would have to understand her goals.

She read her journals from beginning to end; she was then able to recognize her strength, her inner power. Meka decided to help her by taking Faithful in her room and returned her when she was ready to go back to bed. She was awakened later on by her mother's cries. Startled, she jumped when Nicole began to yell at her about touching her. Lying across her bed, she cradled her as she listened. Only after Nicole was finished, did Meka realize she began to cry with her in her arms. She wanted to protect her from the noise. She tucked her into bed around 8:00 p.m. There was no more screaming or cries; at last, they had a peaceful night.

Meka later went back to Nicole's room to check on her. She was sitting there, looking for different support groups in the area and possibly in Washington DC. She took pages and pages of notes. Meka was surprised at how she had the ability to bounce back. She was once a woman of fear, often in flight away from her reality. Helping Nicole helped Meka find her own strength.

Sitting on her bed, Nicole was unable to express her excitement. She found a support group that actually traveled; members had the options of possible growth in their community with references for employment, schooling, and more. It was everything she needed in order to prove she was the better parent for Faithful.

Meka wrote down the contact information. She sent a quick e-mail to ask for more information. Merely three hours later, she had an application packet of information that she was able to download on her computer. She was ecstatic, amazed, and unsure if they would truly understand her. With the application, she needed to send a short essay explaining who she was, her story, and why she believed that support group would be helpful toward her needs. The next day, Meka gave her all the information and suggested to her to get busy working on the required steps.

Nicole typed a letter that was five hundred words long. She asked Meka to proofread it twice. Each time, she became more nervous about her past. She was shy but honest about her trademarks that she had left on this earth. She sent the application in and waited. Hours passed before she received a conformation e-mail. Seven business days passed before she received an emailed response that read, *We would like to thank you for your interest in our support group, but we do not believe the support structure we offer is something that would be beneficial for your needs. However, we do have a reference list of other support groups that may be what you are looking for.*

Somewhat discouraged, she read through the list of support groups, and only a few caught her eye. She again sent in her revised five hundred word essay after she removed a few details. Only one responded to her, and they set up a time to meet; her appointment was two weeks from that day's date at a city hall office. With nothing more to think about, she accepted and picked out her best business attire.

Staring in a daze of confusion, her head began to hurt from the actual thought that this could really happen. Lost in the moment, she began to have a waking nightmare. Standing still, she flashbacked to a time in her life that she was not able to mentally escape. It happened one evening when most were having dinner; she was trapped in a movement of unwanted sexual encounters. Forced into sucking his dick, she was also forced into touching and putting objects in his anus. She had moments when the air would collapse her lungs, not allowing air to enter or exit from her body. Her brain lost track of the actual thoughts; she forgot where she was, who she had become, and what she was doing.

The beatings came and knocked her off her feet. He slapped her hard enough to awaken the dreadful thought that this could be her reality still. She fell to the floor. Blood dripped from her mouth as her lips swelled. Grabbing the carpet to balance herself, she was pushed to the ground. He jumped on top of her; he was deliberate on the gag of his manhood inside her mouth. He jerked himself into her mouth. His hands tied the knot tighter around her wrists, cutting off the blood circulation, and he slowed down his motions. He wanted a reaction from her, yet she laid still. Unable to move, unwilling to give him what he wanted, she closed her eyes and gave in to his demand. Lying limp, she was a prey caught in a predator's mouth. His teeth clutched down on her flesh, but there was still no reaction. He left her to deal with the abuse, the bruises, and the blood left on her mouth. She was left waiting for someone, anyone to free her arms from the scarf that held her bound to a stranger's bed. When freedom finally came, there were more restless actions being forced on her.

Needing to clean herself, she was taken into a room that was known for its horrid odor. The stench could kill the natural minerals; however, the formula was used on "the workers" to kill the leftovers of the johns and John Doe's. This was their way to secure cleanliness. Standing outside, they were lined up against a wall, backs facing the water hose they held on them. They sprayed their bodies with cold bleach water; chills covered the surface of her flesh. It was no surprise that in the winter some had gone into shock. The sex trade game was nothing more than a poker game with one winner in control, the dealer. The memory froze her.

Faithful touched her leg. "Mommy, you okay?"

Awakened from her nightmare, she discovered the tears that

crawled out of her eyes. That was then and this is now. It was a new day, a new way of life, a new opportunity at success.

Nicole began to pack for their future.

Twelve hours later, she and Faithful were in the sky above the clouds. She had made a decision, and it was final. Their boarding passes were in hand, and they were off. They landed in Miami, Florida, at 5:00 a.m. where they were welcomed by heat. It was eighty degrees, and the morning had yet to begin. She grabbed their bags, and they jumped in a Super Yellow Cab. Nicole was headed to the Westin Hotel and Resort. The bright lights, fast cars, and tall buildings were more exciting than she could image. Arriving there was a dream. There were doormen and women stationed at each door ready to hold the door for them. The concierge rushed to grab their luggage and carried it to the front desk for her. Checking in was swift. Everything was ready for them. Her key was ready with her name on it. The Westin was a dream come true for her, and she hadn't even made it to her room yet. The room was on the tenth floor, with a balcony looking over the ocean. Walking into the room, she was amazed at the beds and the comfort. Their new future offered endless possibilities.

She put Faithful to bed and showered in a private shower, allowing the music to sing to her from the surround sound speakers mounted in the bathroom walls. Jazz and a hot, steamy shower! The sun rose before she allowed the water to stop flowing over her head; she gratefully found herself at peace. She wrapped herself in a white robe and rested in her bed.

Chapter 18
Roundup

The party last night was sick. It was the way they wanted to start this journey off. All eyes on them! It was like a kindergarten roundup. On to the next city. Miami, baby! Sandy beaches, warm to hot weather every day. More hotels than any one city can handle. The ladies were excited. *Westin Diplomat Resort and Spa!* It's where they would stay until the meeting was complete. Then they and the final contestants would lay nearly nude on South Beach. They were drinking Wet Willies; slushies for adults made with sour apple and 150-proof alcohol. The taste was different, but the aftereffect was what they needed. Their second meeting would have three applicants, a younger group to challenge them. They would entice the older men; the older, the richer, and the better.

Jojoba Essence's women had a six o'clock flight. Packing was hell, but they were almost done. That was it; Miami Convention Center and 8:00 p.m. could not come fast enough. Getting on the plane was annoying. Salina understood babies were what made the world go round, but what she couldn't understand was why their parents put them on airplanes so early in life, especially a five-hour flight. The family with the baby sat right behind her and Punani Princess. They looked at each other and laughed. Her head was still killing her from the night before. Too much New Amsterdam could do anyone in. She popped two Excedrin and dozed off. Salina could hear the other ladies laughing and reminiscing over their actions of last night. Shining their bracelets in the sunlight, they laughed some more.

The plane ride was like a jump-off for Miami. Salina's concern was a darn hurricane. The last thing she wanted to happen was for water to come clean them out; that would be a catastrophe. They were in the air and the skies were clear, and there was absolutely no turbulence. That was all that mattered. She was ready to feel the fire across her skin. She loved the heat. These ladies had no idea what was in store for them.

Two hours into the flight, the baby did exactly what they thought would happen; he got restless. She wanted to smack the mother for not carrying Benadryl to help ease his pain in this glorifying sunshine. Salina was left to do her best and not flip out. Instead, she offered her services because her large breasts came in handy. She rested him on her breasts and rocked. She figured he was tired and so were the rest of the riders. He must have been tired of his mother, because he fell immediately to sleep. She handed him back to his mother and fell asleep herself. Salina rested her eyes until the flight attendants were telling her to sit her seat upright and to put her seatbelt on. She thought of loyalty, the best word to use in their business. She began putting their next adventure in motion as she was leaving the plane.

The heat hit her as she crossed the threshold of the plane. She smiled. The ladies were moving too slow, and Salina was ready for something cool to drink and warm to eat. Today, they would cab it. Super Yellow Cab lived outside the Miami International Airport; the ladies grabbed two and rode off with the heat to their backs.

Cameras were flashing everywhere. The driver was so busy being worried about what was going on with the cops at the light, they missed their turn. She wanted to say something but decided against it. The best part was a flat-rate of fifty-two dollars. Not a cent more or less. So, she sat back and let him do the driving. First stop, Westin Diplomat Resort and Spa. Second was a luxuriating shower, and third was a leisurely long walk on the beach alone. No matter what crew, group, and friendship that a woman forms, she will always need alone time. Hell, a woman sometimes sits in the bathroom long enough to get that peace of mind back. A long walk on the beach would give her that. The waves were splashing against the shore, and she could see them from the cab as they turned the corner, getting off of I-95 South. She had only a few hours before the moon would be seen in the sky.

Checking in was as usual, smooth. She handed them their card for all three rooms. Fifty-dollar hold for all three. Salina wanted to check on their next set of contestants. Nicole checked in; however, Salina had received a voicemail informing her that Satin and Falisha's plane was going to arrive late, making them late in return. Before walking off, she asked the desk clerk to contact her when the other ladies of their party were ready to check in, no matter the time. She didn't want them to see her, but she wanted to see them.

Jennifer, the front desk agent, knew the drill. She was a closet member herself. She wanted in, but she was too afraid to apply. But, Salina kept her under her wing.

Once the other ladies settled into their rooms, Salina was off for some alone time. She called home to let her husband know how things were going and to let him know she loved him. It was different having a husband who understood her love of great sex and beautiful lovemaking. She kept her word; no sex without him. It tickled her when he would ask, *Who's been sucking my pussy?* She disliked that word, and he knew it. Yet, he insisted on using it. She would respond with, *Yoni has not been touched yet,* and then laugh. The sneakiness in her always came out to shine with that statement. No matter how many degrees he earned teasing about his pussy, her yoni was like playing with her life. He knew it turned her out for him to keep that part of their life alive. The hood is where they rose from; they just chose not to fall there.

While she was lost in thought, he said, "Baby, baby, did you hear me? Don't play with my pussy. You're only a ticket away." He laughed.

"What are you doing tonight?" she asked, changing the subject.

He hated when she asked a question she knew the answer to; it was poker night with the fellows and strippers. His day-off activities happened if she was there or not. He called it his "me time". She smiled at the thought.

"Baby, I'm getting my stuff on so I can take a walk. I want to watch the sun come up around me. I'll give you a call when I get back into my room."

Walking on the beach, the sand was her foundation, her salvation, just like Jesus is for many. Salina ran until her chocolate legs could no longer handle the beating she was forcing on them. Just when she thought she couldn't take any more, it started to drizzle salty rain on her flesh. The mixture of her sweat and the rain pushed her, and she found a new form of energy. It surged through her pores, and she ran faster and harder. She ran until she came upon a young woman and a man, who seemed to be wrestling in the water. Unsure of what she should do next, she watched and waited. She watched, and to her surprise, they were totally engrossed in a steamy lovemaking session. She didn't look for it; it just seemed to fall in her lap. The encounters found her, and she happened to enjoy them. While he was carrying her out of the water, she wrapped her legs around his waist, and he laid her on the blanket hidden behind a palm tree and umbrella.

The mood was perfect for them. No one was supposed to be outside in the middle of their music-less sex scene. But, she was. They captured her attention with the silky blue blanket they lay on. He wrapped her legs around his neck and found heaven within her earth. He was doing something she was unprepared for. She tried to move his head and arms. Holding on tight, he inhaled all of her. The wetness he caused was merely the beginning to an end that should never happen. He tasted her womanhood, sliding a finger inside of her; he pleasured himself with the idea this was the best she had ever had. It was truly his moment to shine. Three fingers later, she was his personal monkey. Two fingers within her vagina, one in her ass, and his mouth on her breast. He was causing heat to rise around the rain that fell on their cool skin.

The water rushed the shore as if trying to touch their surface. It was obvious they were not going to stop; she wanted to pass them, but she also wanted to watch them. Her stomach jumped when she noticed him watching her. Rubbing the woman's thighs, he got her attention; she turned on his command and their pace slowed. Salina thought they were going to stop and yell at her. Instead, they got up and went back into the water; they rinsed off, giving her plenty of time to move along with her journey. She couldn't move; Salina was lost in their actions. It was like an episode of Jojoba Essence all over again!

Sitting there, she dreamt a small dream of them offering for her to join, invading their time. What else was she supposed to think when they were not embarrassed of their actions? It was a natural thought, at least for her. She finally moved on. She wanted them to share their story with her; however, she ran back toward her hotel.

Jogging back, the rain fell harder; she became more concerned for the other contestants. She checked her messages when she got back to her room. Salina didn't want any mishaps on this trip. As she reached the lobby, Salina saw a young woman with a child; a small girl. *Could she be?* She resembled the woman who she knew as Nicole. She checked her out, how she handled herself, how she dealt with her daughter, and the strange space she was in. If she was impressed with this luxurious hotel, she hid it well. Salina thought, *Smart girl.* No one likes a girl who is not used to anything. She didn't speak loudly. In fact, she didn't speak at all, and she carried herself like she knew where she was and what she wanted. Salina was impressed. Looking over her shoulder, she noticed her reflection in the painting; she brushed the bottom of her clothing and moved on to the elevators. Salina wondered what she was doing in the lobby so late at night. Her daughter was quiet enough to the point that if you did not see her, you would not know she was there. Well-behaved! Waiting for her to get on the elevator, Salina walked to the desk to check her messages.

There were no messages! None! Now she was worried. She checked to see if the ladies had checked in; they had not. No calls, no messages, and they were nowhere to be found. She rounded up a few ladies to inform them of her concerns. She needed someone to make calls while she took a shower. Salina was hoping they'd chickened out so she could get some well-deserved rest. It was now 2:00 a.m., and she was exhausted.

Just as she finished her last statement, she turned the shower on. She waited because she wanted the water to be extremely hot when she entered the shower. Her thoughts would not allow her to relax. So, she hopped in the shower, hoping it would calm me. Taking out her apricot body wash, she decided not to use her washcloth. She squeezed a quarter-sized amount into her hands and rubbed her shoulders first. The exfoliating beads in the body wash were exactly what she needed on her flesh. It seemed to scratch away the irritation that her body was experiencing; the rougher she dug, the better it felt. So, she decided why stop there. She stood by the wall and rinsed the soap off her back. The heat began to choke her. Facing the wall, she inhaled and exhaled deeply. The bubbles were surrounding her feet and the steam was above her head.

Before she took her third breath, she heard a knock on her door. She wanted to ignore it, but they wouldn't stop. The irritation was back. *My ladies, they're a lost cause; I love them, but I want to be alone at this moment.* For her own sanity, she needed to get some sleep; she told them all to get some rest, and she'd deal with the situation in the morning. *After all, I would be no good to anyone with a bad attitude from a lack of rest.*

She called the front desk, requesting they give her a wakeup call if they heard anything. She turned the lights out and promptly fell asleep.

Chapter 19
Nicole

Taking a stroll on the beach at night was wonderful, with the breeze and the salt in the air. It was magnificent, a peace of mind that everyone should enjoy at least once. The sand was soft between her toes and the moon was over the ocean. She was breathless. She had found her home, and she was not even looking for it. Her God had answered her prayers, just when she didn't know what to pray for. Faithful seemed to be at peace as much as she was. She had not said a word for a while; Nicole assumed she was exhausted and ready for bed. Heading back to the hotel, she decided to stop in the lobby.

Nicole came in just in time, because the rain began falling just as the doors closed behind her. Faithful was clinging to her leg like Saran wrap. She was unsure if she was scared or if she was tired. She was beginning to believe she was there alone because there were no messages for her. No other ladies in the lobby looked like they were in need of a support group.

Heading to the elevators, she could feel the presence of someone behind her and stopped to look in the mirror to see if she could see them. Fixing her clothing, she noticed a lady, who appeared to be in her early thirties watching her. Nicole grew concerned because she watched as if she had something to say to her; instead, she remained silent and watched her from afar. Hoping she was not giving any obvious idea that she was watching the woman in the same manner, she continued to the elevator. She held Faithful's hand a little firmer. She went upstairs to her room and tucked her baby in. Watching her baby sleep was peaceful. Nicole was able to protect her and deceive her father at the same time. This was her new home, and tomorrow would show that her past was no longer an obstacle for her future.

10:00 a.m.

The sun was high in the sky, and the heat suppressing itself around flesh as she walked around the corner at the Miami Convention Center. The area was beautiful. Taking the shuttle south down A1A, she was amazed at the traffic and the extravagant homes. All the gated communities were perfectly symmetric, with squared bushes that did not allow common individuals to gaze over the hedges. As the bus picked up and dropped off passengers, Nicole wondered how such an extravagant place existed. The traffic was mildly packed. No one was getting in or out of the lanes. Forty-five minutes later, the bus passed a car accident. *Rushing to the beach,* she thought! Faithful was sleeping in her arms; the heat had wiped her out.

Less than an hour later, they arrived at the Miami Convention Center. The Botanical Garden was across the avenue. Nicole searched for a moment of peace before entering the center. So, she walked across to the garden and walked until she had found the courage to move forward. Walking and praying had always soothed her. This was their moment! She knew she had to take this opportunity. Nicole knew who she was, where she was, and where she was going to be. This was her time and she was going to take it. The sun was still high in the sky, yet she felt sprinkles on her flesh. It was as if her archangel Michael was crying for her strength.

Approaching the door, the doorman reached out for Faithful. She stepped back and questioned his motives. Her exact words were, "Excuse me, what the fuck is wrong with you!"

He apologized. "Ma'am, the other ladies have gathered in the other room, and I was instructed to take her to the daycare area of the center, if that's okay with you, so you're not late. If you're late, they will lock the doors. You still need to place your blindfold on. The daycare is on the basement level. It was requested for me to help you and your daughter."

Accepting what he said, she released her daughter to this stranger. Nicole was nervous, but it was a support group meeting. What could happen? Walking through the double-glassed doors, she was approached by another gentleman. He placed the black blindfold on her, which was totally unexpected. Following suit, Nicole allowed him to guide her to her seat. She could hear talking and mumbling.

Nicole became frantic at the thought of what she had gotten herself involved in. Just then, she whispered to God, "Heavenly Father, I ask that you protect me and my daughter as you have always done. Jesus, in your name I pray for your continuous protection. Amen."

A voice came over the loudspeaker as she finished her prayer.

"I would like to thank each of you for your consideration and support of our journey. I would like each of you to take a moment to introduce yourselves. I will start, and when I am finished, I will touch the person to my right. So on and so on until a person touches me on my shoulder.

"Hello, my name is Jojoba. I created this group for women alike to express themselves openly and honestly. We are a sisterhood on many levels. We are a group of women who are independent in life. Some have a husband, some are part of the GLBT community, and others are single and enjoy it just the same. I am married and have no children, and that is okay with me."

Listening to her, she was beautiful. Her voice kept an even tone, never too loud, and she sounded confident. Nicole was nervous all over again.

What will I say? she thought. *I am a result of a teen pregnancy. I landed in foster care and was then put on the streets of Minnesota because my foster parent was sure I was sleeping with her husband. Never confirmed it, but I was certain that was the reason. The state paid for me to be there and I worked, so they kept all the money. Maybe I could tell them that I was a part of the sex trade industry for two years. I was saved by a man and then became pregnant by him and was placed in a community for homeless teen parents.*

She was tapped on her shoulder. She had missed everyone else's story. Sighing, she took a breath that lasted longer than she anticipated.

"My name is Nicole, and I have a daughter and her name is Faithful. My reason for joining this support group is to provide my child with a childhood that I was unable to have. There was no support for my mother which led to her early demise. I will open doors for my daughter because I am opening doors for myself. By any means necessary, my child will have a quality of life that she and every child deserves. I was born in Minnesota and experienced much of my trauma there."

Nicole heard laughter. Her heart sank.

Salina quickly spoke up. "This is a group for mature women. We have come from all walks of life, and the chance that any one of us could possibly walk in the next person's shoes and survive is unlikely."

Giving weight to their laughter, Nicole's self-esteem had been injured, but she ended her introduction with, "Your laughter is only cause for me to succeed."

Nicole tapped the next person on the shoulder, and she began to speak. "My name is Annette. I am a recent divorcee of a year. I smile because it was never meant, but we tried anyway. I am a lesbian woman with a sensual taste for life in every sense. When I was honest with my husband, it was like I met the perfect stranger. He smiled at me and said, 'I know you are a woman of great things, but a woman of secrets you have never been'. We hugged, we kissed, and we made love. He touched me, and I caressed him. Lying still, I knew I loved him, and I desired for him to be happy. However, I was more enticed with the idea of me being happy for the first time in my life. We still love and will probably always love one another. Yes, I think about us often and wonder did I make the right decision. But, I know I did. He is now married and in love with a woman that has borne his first child, something I could never give him.

"Today, I am in love with a woman that I may never have, but I love her just the same. She presented me with a printout of the information of the support group. Looking in my eyes, she said, 'Maybe then you will understand'. Because I want to understand her, I am here. I am here because this is her home away from home. She never speaks of things she does, yet she always has a look in her eye that I would love to have."

Assuming she was done, the room became silent. Another lady began to speak. Nicole mind began to wonder. She thought about her daughter. She couldn't hear her crying or playing. *Was she safe? Was she hungry? Is she asleep? Is there food available for her to eat?* Jojoba began to speak and interrupted Nicole's thoughts. "Thank you all for your introductions. Now that we have come to an understanding of why and what we want from this journey, it's time. Please take a moment and answer these questions silently. "How do you feel about sex? How does it affect you? Must you be in control at all times; are you submissive when the time is right? Do you fulfill fantasies with your mate? Your honesty will lead you to the next level, or it will lead you out the door. Either way, it is your honesty and your right. If your answer to the first question is, I can live with or without it you should leave. If you believe your past has taken a toll on your sex life, and you have negative thoughts about sex, then you should leave."

Nicole shifted, but stayed. *Submissive never again,* she thought. *In control, I would love to be in control of my sexual desires. To demand and command for someone to do things that I like. To piss on their back as they did to me, I would love to choke him because it excites him.* This realization became exciting to her.

Then, Salina said something that was obvious to the truth of who she was. Nicole was a pleaser. She had fulfilled enough fantasies to save a lifetime. Nicole was curious to what any of this had to do with what she had in mind, but she listened. She went on to say, "This is a group for exposure of the male sex. We as women have a place in history, where we are giving what we have been getting for years. We are taking the actions against men that have been happening to women for centuries, and this time you get to choose to participate. Can I see a hand of the individuals who are willing to take a stand against men and the bullshit they have given us as women?"

Nicole's hand went in the air before she could take another breath. Salina was inspirational. Nicole felt empowered by the idea of taking back her strength that she lost years ago. She thought, *you laughed because my success causes fear to settle in your heart*. The room's walls began to wail. The roaring of the women in the room was overwhelming for one lady. She yelled, "I am not interested in a man-hate group. I love my husband; I was interested in something to get me out the house once a week, not something that will make me go home and hate him."

Silence fell upon the room again. The door opened and then closed. With the blindfold on she naturally thought, *one down*. Jojoba asked, "Is there anyone else who feels we are teaching the hate of our beautiful men?" Salina said, "I love my husband the same way. But that does not stop me from wanting to please myself while pleasing him. Honesty; that is what will keep the group successful and happy. If you feel that way, it is okay. That's why we keep blindfolds on until the conclusion of the meeting; to protect the current members of our group, you will sign a disclosure contract. So know this group is death before dishonor in every sense. Ask yourself again, is this something you are interested in doing?"

No one moved. It was in unison that we sighed from relief as Jojoba went on to give more details. No more principles of the group stated they hated men. A chill went down Nicole's spine when she said they had to sign their contracts in blood. She thought to herself, *how dramatic*. Again, they were given the choice to leave. Nicole's blood began racing to the pit of her hand, she could feel her success. Maybe she was confused about the feeling she had. Either way, she didn't move. Nicole stayed and signed her name. They removed their blindfolds and the women were beautiful. To her surprise, they were much older than her. They had this way of swaying across the room. They hugged and laughed, some drank alcoholic beverages, and others just embraced their new family members.

Jolting toward the door, Nicole went to find her daughter. It had been over an hour, and she wanted to be sure she was okay. Watching her rest gave Nicole a sense of relief. She was napping in the children's play area. The journey of Jojoba Essence was their beginning. This was their moment. The awakening of the new her was enlightening, and she had several drinks. Empowered with strength, she no longer feared her future or Faithful's father.

Running back upstairs, it was time for part two. Roll call as they called it. Every woman had to come up with a new name, something sexy, erotic and it must fit their true personality. Standing in the circle, women were getting very creative thinking of their new names.

There were names Nicole would have never thought of, such as Anal this, Pussy that, and more. Annette chose Lick Her Love, which Nicole found intriguing. The ghetto crew, as Nicole called them, called themselves the Double Knot. They are tag-teamers. Nicole was still pondering names as they were writing the names down and signing their contracts. Then it was her turn, she pondered and thought and thought. Those few minutes seemed like hours. She wanted to pass, but she was the last one. The room was waiting on her, and the best thing she could think of was water. Wet like water, but that wasn't a name; it was a statement. She decided on Fluent. Fluent because she has skills beyond her wildest dreams; she loves it and hates it. Her past opened doors for her in a way she never imagined.

She is *Fluent.*

Fluent? Fluent? This would most definitely have to grow on her or not; MIMS showed her that she had the ability to be fluent in her everyday life. Fluent it is. Then she signed. The prick was not horrible but painful enough. They toasted! Miami was a city of hopes and dreams, even for those who come from afar. Twelve hours later, Nicole was pooped. She was ready to go back to her room, but the conference room had filled with strangers; men, and lots of them. They were of all shades, Dominican, White, and Black-African.

The ladies gathered in one circle. Jojoba offered the men as a treat to their union. Glasses in the air, and Lick Her Love said, "What about me?" The door chimed. Turning to the sound, they watched as a flood of extraordinary women flowed in. She smiled tapped their glass and left the circle. They all laughed. Somehow, one caught her eye and wouldn't let go of it. Jojoba pulled Nicole to the side, and asked, "Is everything okay?" Nicole expressed that she was open to the event, but she had no idea what to do next. Jojoba said, "Go with the flow. Never say yes and never say no. Stay in control and focus. You are Fluent, now flaunt it."

Chapter 20
Ghetto Girls: Keshia and Teshia

That plane ride was ridiculous. The damn pilots fell asleep! Either way, they went right over Miami and wound up somewhere over the ocean, when the pilots finally acknowledged what the hell was going on. Babies, along with their mothers were crying, and people were sweating. Every thought in the world was being spoken if they were dead; people were drinking, wondering if they were going to kill us, or if the plane had been hijacked. The stories went on and on, until the flight attendant came over the loudspeaker and tried to reassure everyone that they were safe. "United West has flown all day, and there is no reason to be alarmed."

Thirty minutes later, the plane was turning around. This had to be some kind of a joke. They had their trip planned to an exact science. They should be jumping in the ocean; instead, they had headaches because of poor planning. The sun should be bathing their skin, and the salt of the ocean should be drying their skin out. Instead, they were stuck here on this overcrowded jumbo jet, with the smells of who knows what crawling around. Frustrated does not begin to touch the tip of their emotions. It was another hour before they were finally on the landing strip of Miami International Airport.

5:00 a.m.

Arriving at the Westin Diplomat Resort Hotel was the best part of the trip so far. Their feet were tired and their heads ached. As twins do, they shared in the agonizing pain of the flight. They were pissed; they lost half a day of their trip. Getting checked in was another hassle. They walked in, and there was a slum-looking family the counter. They had a dog that was nothing more than a mutt. The family had scrapes and bruises all over. Blood was creeping down their legs, arms, and other parts of their body. What bothered them the most was that the hotel personnel didn't keep them from sitting on the furniture. Keisha looked at her with the same disgusting look, as she was thinking; *waiting in the sitting area was a near-death situation. Hell, we don't know if this trailer trash family has AIDS or any other blood-borne disease.*

This day just keeps fucking getting better. Seeming simple enough, a trip that should have taken six hours, took a long ten hours. The only accommodations that they offered were a free ride to their destination. Her fear was that their room was no longer available. They wondered if the support group thought they weren't coming. This was a mess. They had multiple messages from the lady they spoke with over the phone. She was acting like a worried mother, asking if they were okay, wondering if they were still coming, and reassuring them that if they didn't come, it was okay but she would like a phone call to let her know what they were going to do. When they got to the desk to check in, there were more messages left there. To put an end to what the day had started off for them, they treated this as a lesson learned. Do not travel unless they were driving. Because she had not heard from them, the meeting was changed to 10:00 a.m., which meant that they could get a few more hours of sleep.

They were only steps away from their room when they heard a noise. The situational chaos from earlier was behind them as they looked for their rooms. When they found it, Keisha dropped her bags and opened the door. The room was kind of small for their liking; cozy but small. It was updated with all the right equipment, but was pricey, and there was not enough room to run. Their luggage was too close to them, and the closet was too small for two people. Besides, who in the hell charges for Internet services in a hotel these days? They could go to a coffee shop and get it free. Then the bar was another thought; three dollars for a can of pop. What the hell ever. Even the richest of the rich don't buy that shit.

They shared a view out of this world; they were on the ninth floor, and the ocean was marvelous, genuine in its nature. Her sister was in the shower steaming out the bathroom. Her mother called her Precious as a child, because she was so slow. She moved as if the world waited on her. The clock could knock on the door, and she would not move any faster than what pace she was at. That was annoying. Dealing with authority was never her best quality either. Choosing a life of freedom has cost them; their trust funds have been on hold until they return to school and give up on their entrepreneurial voyage. Researching on Bing gave them great ideas, but then they stumbled upon the site for support groups.

Being five-one and fair-skinned with dark black hair, most would mistake them as white girls. On the contrary; they were Black women who were adopted by their mother and father when their biological mother was carrying them. She was the typical high school girl. From the footage that they have seen of her, she is a remarkable woman. Her success is her claim to fame; she was an actress of all things! She knew she could never become more than she was with a set of twins; a single mother on welfare, maybe with a two-year liberal arts degree. Maybe a nurse, but not her true heart's desire, which was to be an actress. Coming from Newark, New Jersey, she feared failure. There was no way she was going to let two children stop her stride towards her future. Her downfall was a blessing to a couple who couldn't have children. It was an open adoption, which meant she had the right to visit on the holidays and birthdays, and to send letters and gifts. Her entourage was the people they often saw with her, but it was fair because their mother and father loved them as much if not more than she did.

Their mother was proud of their achievements and their decision of becoming entrepreneurs together. However, their mother and father felt otherwise. Their parents' enthusiasm was hidden by fear and sadness. Somehow they were able to make this about not loving them. It wasas if to say the only way to show and prove that their love was enough was to do exactly what they wanted. They couldn't explain it enough to them that that's not love and it's not happiness. They taught them to stand up for themselves, go after what they wanted, and do not allow anyone to hold them back. All of their lives that's what they heard and now their parents make them feel guilty. The twins' trip gave them an insight on what they needed to do. Either they would go back to school or they would move forward on their dreams as entrepreneurs. Time would tell.

Arriving at the meeting, they were sure they were going to see a different atmosphere. On the contrary; they couldn't see anything. Jojoba's voice sounded like the age of our parents.

Then, the chick next to them started to tell her story as if they were on Oprah. Streaming tears released from her eyes and no one budged. They didn't even pass her a napkin. *"What the fuck? Who cares if she was homeless? That she had a child; don't they offer birth control for people on welfare? It was apparent she was or is on welfare and this crowd of women was too much for her to handle".* Snickering, Keisha said, "I bet she has never ridden a dick. Missionary sex is her best action. Her name should never be Fluent. Fluent in what, Spanish? Straight A's and one B havin'-ass bitch. Her lips barely fit her face. One big bottom lip and thin top lip. Bitch sucks a dick, never! Eat pussy is more like it." Keisha wouldn't let up.

One thing about my sister is once she gets going, there is less of a chance I will be able to stop her. Being identical twins caused chaos for the both of us. She snickered and I intensely stared at her. But then, the lady over the loudspeaker stops the flow of the introduction to remind us about being adults. Wrong foot again! I just cut my eyes at Keisha. She couldn't see me but she felt me squeeze her hand. Keisha had the ability to piss me off at times with her immaturity. Teshia withered at the thought of Keisha being in this life without her. They are a pair never to be separated. Loving her sister was not a duty, however, it is difficult at times. Unfortunately, they are identical twins and they are paired together even when one chooses not to be. Being scolded for her behavior upset her stomach. She felt like a child. She was almost embarrassed for her sister's actions and more importantly, her own actions for not controlling her reaction to ignorance. It's one thing to have those feelings but it's another to respond. Nonetheless, they are here and ready for a teaching.

Keisha wanted to learn how to ride a dick better than she knew how to milk a cow. Teshia thinks that sucking the skin off a penis is what she wants to do. Gag reflex expert. She loves the idea of controlling a man through the slip of her tongue. She gets off from watching their toes curl, watching them pull the covers around them. She likes the lights on and them looking her in the eyes. She wanted the memory of her mouth to linger with them as they went on about their day. She laughed every morning after they went for breakfast, never with him, but with her sister to share in her whorish glory.

Keisha loves riding dick. Discovering the cowgirl and reverse cowgirl was like shining a new light on her life. Her sister once watched her sexing one of her boyfriends and she had one leg in the air another wrapped around his neck. They were ninety degrees across the bed. She would say, "I can be his slut while being his African queen."

When roll call came around to her, she chose a name that fit her well; "Ride 'Em Right". Her sister settled on "Long and Strong". With glasses high in the air, this was a toast to remember. It was final and all papers were signed and sealed.

Chapter 21
Let's Dance

The party started with men walking in. Keisha found Mr. Dark Chocolate and Teshia found Mr. Swirl. Teshia and Mr. Swirl fought from the start. Their tongues wrestled until they fell to the cushioned carpet. He rolled her across the floor until the burns were more than they could handle. The next time she looked up, she was a pretzel. The heels of her feet were touching her forehead and she was in heaven with his tongue deep inside her ass. He licked her like she was a butter pecan ice cream cone, and he was looking for her nuts. The more she was deeply involved in her encounter, the more her sister wanted to become involved in her own.

Mr. Dark Chocolate was different. They paced themselves assuming they had all night. They had a few more drinks, and talked about all the things that didn't matter in the situation they were in. The passion was truly there, but the chemistry was too strong. He appeared to be looking for his Mrs. Right, and she was honestly looking for Mr. Right Now. Keisha wanted to pull him to the back stairwell area, and have him ride her over the banister. Maybe slip down the stairs as he doubled over her to find her spot. Her G-spot was difficult to find. She has a tilted cervix, and it hides behind it. She was losing interest with all the extra talking. She was intrigued for sure, but she figured she was not on a formal date and didn't want to be. Keisha wanted to learn, but not about him, more so about the position he has had women in and what positions he has wanted to try. She thought, *"Shit, I am flexible, and he should know that by now."* She leaned in and kissed him on his lips. She couldn't take it anymore; they looked soft, and she wanted to know if her lip radar was off. By his reaction, she knew he enjoyed what she had done. That was her way of knowing she had to be the dominate one in their situation. In that decision alone, she knew what was to come next.

Keisha demanded for him to fall to his knees. He looked at her as if he wanted to second-guess or question what she was asking of him. She stood to her feet and pointed to the ground right on the side of her. *"I want you here and now; on your knees bitch."* He obeyed and she was surprised. She didn't know she had it in her. It was some sort of a head rush and a turn on to be in control. Taking his belt off his pants, she wrapped one end on her hand and buckled the rest to his neck. Keisha walked him as if she was his Dom. Having control, she had the ability to give the control back to him with one simple command. "Protect me, and be mean about it." He loudly barked, which caused the party goers to become their audience. They were amused at their show. They began clapping; however they were lost in thought and were forced to notice that they had every eye in the room.

Some of the women were knee-deep in sucking whatever dick was in front of them. Women who were taking it from the back were smiling at them. She was interested in him taking advantage of a real good thing, her in this moment. She walked him to the corner of the building that was not being occupied. As they walked past onlookers, he barked continuously. He barked and barked until her pussy began to drip juices down her thighs, and wrapped themselves around her knees. It was if he was a bloodhound seeking something. His aggression became stronger as they passed more onlookers. It came to a point he was pulling her; to her it was his way of taking more control from her.

Just as they reached the door to leave the common area of the convention center, he turned to her and said, "Bitch, your turn." He wanted her silenced, as if she had a muzzle on. For her, this was quite the challenge because she wanted to be seen. Instead, he called attention to them by simply saying to the room behind them, "Look at my bitch. She is the most obedient bitch I have ever had." Speaking loud and strong, he tapped her on her ass and said, "Good girl. Good girl." He said, "Watch this" to the room. He fell to his knees and licked her inner thighs. "You like that?" he asked. She moaned like a puppy in heat. "Good girl," he said again. He stood up and walked around to face her, and he said, "You want more." She moaned some more, and heard another "Good girl." He looked her in the eyes, and demanded for her to stand. She got on her knees. He said, "Good girl."

Just as she thought this moment of sexual insanity was almost over, he removed the belt from her neck and said, "That's my bitch, now sit." Bending over, he lifted her and turned her upside down, and he ate her pussy standing. Not sure how it happened or even when but her panties were off, and she was sucking his dick. The audience they had was so involved in what they were doing, they forgot about their own interactions. His tongue was in her pussy, his manhood in her mouth and his fingers deep in her vagina as his tongue played with her clit. *And he said he was a vegan.* She no longer believed that shit. His dick was nine inches long, one and a half inches thick, and beautiful. Not too long and not too short; a nice size around, who could ask for more? With them standing underneath the light above the door, their onlookers could see the moisture from his mouth run over her ass cheeks. His moisture and her wetness caused a glossy stain over her ass.

At one point in time, she could feel a teardrop size puddle of wetness run down the middle of her back and stop at the nape of her neck. Her ass was crying, and it felt more than wonderful. That moment felt as if it lasted at least an hour. As the blood rushed to her head, he flipped her back to where her tongue found his lips again. She was ready to put him to the test. Her pussy was ready for him to devour it, to caress it with the tip of his manhood. Folding her in half, he lifted her in the air against his flesh. The tip of her toes barely touched the floor. Considering she was five-four and one hundred and sixty pounds, she didn't see how he could do it. But he did, and didn't miss a beat.

Mr. Dark Chocolate was busy at work before he noticed that the room was circling them. The passion they shared was immaculate. The heat from the circle around them was outstanding. One couple came close enough to touch her breasts. Another couple lay beneath their feet, and the man started to touch himself. Truthfully, she didn't know how long they were going, but she was dizzy. The condom was hanging from the tip of his penis, and her pussy was yearning to be left alone. Lying on the floor next to the people nearest to them, she inhaled and allowed her exhaustion to exhale. Out of breath, he fell to his knees and cradled her. He fucked with passion and anger. He was mad and she wanted to know why. Or did she?

She thought, *I didn't cause the conflict he held within, yet I benefited the most*. There must be some truth to his thoughts. He was a warrior. His deep stroke was immaculate. When he pushed his dick inside of her, his body weight fell against her as well. The longer he went, the more she wanted his body heat. The underlining fact was she could never fuck this man again; a rule of thumb in this business was that a person could never get attached. *You never go back.* He could fuck all the sisters in their sisterhood next and there would be nothing she could do about it.

When the strength came back into her knees, she walked to the restroom and cleaned herself. It was fully stocked with FDS spray, wipes, and cream to cool their vaginas. Walking into the restroom, she noticed out the corner of her eye he was talking with Jojoba. She wondered what they were talking about. She just wanted to clean herself and get some refreshments. Turning to dry her hair, she paused as Jojoba walked in and hugged her. Jojoba said, "I would announce it later, but you are the grand prize winner of the evening." With a puzzled look on her face, she thanked her and continued to dry her hair. Jojoba had somewhat of a dismayed look on her face, so Keisha asked her what was wrong. With no response, she handed her five thousand dollars. She began to explain, "We never tell about the money of the night because we want it to be fair game." Whoever does their best win, simple! Some nights we have multi-winners, other times we just split the money, and some nights no one takes the money, then it builds for their next encounter. However, tonight *Ride 'Em Right* took the pot. *I almost felt like a high-class, paid escort.* She would reveal the winner at the next meeting, and that's how it went.

One month would pass before anyone would know. She ended the conversation with, "You cannot win again for six months, great performance or not, we want everyone to feel like a winner." As soon as Jojoba exited the restroom her sister entered; she must have been waiting outside the door. Keisha began to dry her hair again.

"What were y'all talking about?"

"How well he was fucking me."

The difference between fucking in a room and fucking in front of a crowd is that a person cannot lie down; they have to appear as strong as possible. As they left the restroom, her knees tried to bow and fold her in half again but she, like a doe, kept pushing forward. All eyes on her and she felt it.

Reaching the table where the drinks were, he stood there watching her, he asked, "Can we finish our conversation now?" She grinned and allowed him to finish what he was telling her before. Only then did he learn he was thirty-five with a ranch in Northern California. He owned a ski slope and a ton of horses. She wasn't sure why he told her those things, because they would never see one another after this evening was her belief. She asked, "How often do you come to these parties?" "Every chance I get, but this is the first time I have had sexual intercourse with someone; usually, I come to watch and have ideas for when I am ready to devour on a masterpiece." Half-believing and halfway ignoring him, she leaned in and asked something she shouldn't have, and broke one of the biggest rules of their sisterhood. "Are you married?" Cutting his eyes at her, he responded, "Hell, no," as if she offended him with her distasteful question. The look in his eyes made her wish she could have swallowed the words that came out of her mouth, but there was nothing she could do about it. The words were out there, she could only pray he didn't tell Jojoba. She had just gone over the rule book, each page had the words: never ask if the person is married; it's the law.

Saved by the bell! The ending bell rang, giving them ten minutes to say their good-byes and gather their belongings. He leaned into her and apologized for his outburst. Finishing his thought, he gently ran his hand over her face, saying, "I could never do this to a woman I love. I am here to enjoy the life I have built for myself before I get married." Ending their evening at the door he said, I will see you next month." She thought, *how?* She knew they'd get new men each time. *What does he have, some sort of connection or lifetime membership? Who the hell is he?* She watched his back as he entered the stretch Hummer limousine and when the truck pulled off, she was in a trance. She needed something more to drink. Their party started at nightfall, and the party outside was still going and it was daybreak. They could hear the music from clubs. The street lights were flashing, and the moon was high in the sky. The heat wrapped around her thighs and forced her to walk with the ladies down the street to their shuttle bus; Keisha was ready for bed. However, all the ladies who participated in the evening activities were encouraged to get out and shake the men out of their system.

The club BEDS was only a few miles away. Getting in was a long process, but once they were in they found the VIP area. The VIP had beds everywhere. The average attendees had to dance around. After their long evening of sexual freedom, they grabbed a VIP special with two beds and two bottles of Grey Goose which came with flames on top of them. The waiter did his three-drink tricks and they began to drink. Drinking was the beginning but some of the sisters had other things in mind. One of their freaky sisters decided she would invite someone into VIP and sex them with a new audience. People were taking took photos of this fool. By 4:00 a.m., there was nothing anyone could say to her.

Six clubs later, Keisha was pushing her sisters onto the shuttle bus. Ghetto bitches! Everybody had their heels in their hands and crawling on the bus. Sitting at the light, the shuttle guy smiled and said, "Did you all find what you were looking for?"

No one responded. During the ride, Keisha decided she would go for a run on the beach during the morning sunrise.

Chapter 22
Jojoba

"I knew that bringing in younger women would bring in a better form of revenue. One hundred and fifty thousand dollars later, I was able to pocket one hundred of that, paid the bills and slapped our lucky winner with five thousand."

Dark Chocolate signed a year contract with the sisterhood. It was all starting to pay off, the hard work, the lies, the traveling away from home, and Salina missing her husband. She had finally generated more income than she spent for the man she loved. The businessmen who demanded erotic attention was finally taking her husband serious. Dark Chocolate was a different type of guy. He didn't come off like the other creeps; he actually focused on the lady's needs. He actually thought this scam was for the ladies. He was the gold mine Salina was looking for. He was a man of patience and elite posture. He stood five eleven, weighed two hundred and ten pounds of solid muscle, and crepuscular complexion. He moved with grace. Dark Chocolate was beautiful. Selfishly enough, Salina wanted him to herself. He attended eight sessions before he made a move on one of the sisters. There was something about this man; he was a villain. Approached by many and yet he'd slept with none. Many of the sisters thought he was gay. Others wanted Salina to watch out for him; they thought he seemed untrustworthy. Yet, Salina just wanted to ride his thickness and to taste his semen.

He was far from interested. After he attended three sessions, Salina approached him with the sisters' concerns. When she approached him, she rubbed his knee and his back. He simply rejected her. Dark Chocolate gave her a look that suggested she was in his space.

She rose from the stool that she rested on and put her hand out and said, "You seem unpleased with your choices."

He responded by saying, "Choices? I should be their choice."

Smiling at him, she asked, "What are you in search of?"

He said, with a simple grin, "I want a woman who is five-two, dark caramel, hips, and small waist. No breasts and a woman who will follow suit and take control when I give it to her; someone who can take my dick in any form that I give it. She must have the ability to keep my attention from the next pretty face."

Salina's response was simple as his smile. "You are looking for your wife. Not sure if you can find a wife where women belong to someone else. They are here like you but looking for fun. They come here to relieve themselves of their campaign field lives. Their lives are filled with hustle and grizzle. Their children are adults. Their husbands demand more of their wives' attention for his dreams, instead of being challenged for her dreams. These women want to be relaxed with sexual healing, nothing more, and nothing less."

Looking to him, Salina asked, "What do you suppose I do to accommodate your needs?"

Pondering his thoughts, he said, "You do as you may, but I want what I want. My membership will expire with no chance of replacing it or the individuals who accompany me. So think about that, and do your best." He turned his back on her and gathered his belongings while dismissing himself.

She was left to figure it out. Salina had no idea how she would keep their sisterhood's privacy and subdue the bill-payers of the empire. As a businesswoman, she had to think about the entire domain of what she had built. *Would pleasing Dark Chocolate's taste for women be detrimental to the agency as a whole?* The next person to take the lead couldn't know this information. There was no other person she could speak to about her concerns besides her husband. He would know what to do.

One evening over dinner, she brought up her proposed thoughts; to her surprise his suggestion was that she needed to speak with the other members to see if they were willing to take that risk. Salina asked her husband to accompany her to the meeting. Declining her offer, he told her that was a journey she would have to travel alone. She drowned out what he was saying. Salina was annoyed by his way of telling her no. She wanted him to help her. Instead, she was left to deal with it alone. Salina modestly changed the conversation.

Weeks later, she was standing in front of the women, explaining how this would be a good thing. "It would mean lesser fees for us and his membership alone could carry our desires for the next three sessions. He could be responsible for bringing in new meat and the workload would come to an acute halt for us, less lies to tell, and more fun. That's what we are here for, fun and that is what he has guaranteed. We all know that we are tired of finding quality men ourselves. The women we bring in will be a small project that we can work on. They will be younger, and they will need us. Teach them is the model and better our chance of better dick."

That night, they were split. There was a vote and some were certain if the vote passed they would walk. They didn't feel the risk was worth the trouble that could follow. The other half didn't see it like that; they saw dollar signs and more trips with great dick. The vote passed eleven-to-nine. One lady was serious; they lost a sister that evening and gained a new policy. Younger is what they will have, and celibate was the main criteria. One child was the most, and they need sponsors, because they will not have the funds that the others have available to them.

Now they had to find them. "Internet," Elicit screamed. They believed it was feasible so they passed another vote, for an internet social group with benefits. The women thought more about it and the final debate rested on a support group with benefits; this would be appealing to those who were in need of their services. Their promoted purpose was connections throughout the country, a home, career, and the chance at a better life was what they would offer. It was finalized. Uploading the page took the remaining three hours of the meeting.

That evening they lost a sister who has been with them from the beginning, but she had to do what she had to do. Her specialty of sucking a mean dick would truly be missed by the gentlemen. The way she took a man's penis in her mouth was marvelous. She had this way of allowing the head of whatever dick she was servicing to fall down the back of her throat. It became a game to watch how the men's eyes would roll in the back their sockets. The ladies often teased her about receiving lessons, but their request went unanswered. Now she was gone and hadn't taught any of them her tricks. The sisterhood atmosphere was shifting. It was a business and she needed to conduct it as such.

All the fabulous trips, expensive food and drinks were beginning to take its toll on her. She missed her husband. Calling home would be just what she needed. She missed his touch, the smell of their bed sheets, the softness, the biting and hair when he dug in deep from behind; it took her senses to a level of a better love making. When he called her name, it was full of passion. Salina was in need of her husband. She missed his attention to detail when he caressed her face. How he pulled her close to him when they slept. Her husband was predictable. Salina knew Tuesday he was at a meeting from three to five. He would leave there and go for a Cognac at the gentlemen's club. His nightcap relaxed him before he went home. When he left the club, he would give the disc jockey a note asking that the blonde beauty meet him at the door. She would meet him there, give him a hug and kiss him behind his ear, whisper something and he would slide her a hundred dollar bill. She folds it in half and put it in her left breast. Smacking her on her behind, he walked out, drove home and kissed her and asked, "How was your day?" Salina simply missed her husband before he became unpredictable.

At first, the PI was unsure if she wanted to share the information. To her, it was purposeless. No real talking, touching, cuddling, or anything that should have been counted as cheating. But she wanted the pictures. Salina wanted the truth. There was no doubt she loved her husband. Once he became unpredictable he became untrustworthy, so she had him followed. Months later, the pictures were consistent. Every Tuesday, it was the same thing. She could have talked to her or chased her like she was in Eric Jerome Dickey's book *Chasing Destiny*. Salina thought deeply about becoming unladylike, but those actions never suited her well. She thought about taking the string of the tramp's thong and tying her ears together behind her head. She wanted that woman to leave her husband alone. But she couldn't; that was the rule of an open marriage. He had the right, and so did she.

Basically, they were no more than a high-profile swinger party when she was home. He watched and participated in all activities. Being on the road gave her yoni a break from the continuous beat-down he offered it. One more day of this and she would be heading home to a land of hugs and kisses. He wants her to believe that he is faithful, that there is no other woman to take her place. Since the day she married him, he's always said, "You are the one I love, the only beauty that I see and the air that I breathe." That was a lie. He had a black blonde beauty that he kept to himself. They were supposed to share in all goodies. All the fun has somehow marred their marriage, but she would never tell him. There was money to be made now.

In spite of that, his words meet her ears as a rehearsed sermon. The preacher who praise the words he says but doesn't honor them. His ability to illustrate their love is much different since money has become the root to their vacuous love. They were foolish to fall in love with the greater things in life. They should have been comfortable with what they had except for greed. Five years later they were knee deep in money and the love was displaced. Their arguments became settled agreements to save face. They had become business partners. Jojoba Essence is a buttress to the rest of the world, a support system. If they knew the truth, they would have assumed that they were women with no class, but it was more than that; they were women who had desires, feelings, and emotions that were being ignored by the ones they love the most, their husbands. Pleasing their husbands was their glory; it was frame to the name, Jojoba Essence. As for the name, she chose because it was sensual, unknown, and owns much value. Jojoba is oil that is used from head to toe in most body products.

They were the humanistic value of the oil.

Chapter 23
Nicole

The ladies were becoming arrogant. They knew they were the best at what they did. It was exciting, daring, and full of fear and a breath of fresh air. The sex stories that they told with their bodies was emasculate. The aroma from the room was thick; it was strong, and the flame from the candles flickered. The candles were strawberry. Each flame shadowed the bricks that surrounded them. Coolness seeped in through the cracks of the windows and the heat rose between each active body. Nicole had never seen such willing passion. Each person wrestling to be better than the next! Whistling, she kept to herself. She wanted to observe. She learned how to sexually love a man by watching her sisters. She learned how not to allow her mind to become keen on the superficial details; on the contrary, her mind was penetrating, which focused on the underlying causes of everyone's actions. She was aroused to know that one day she could be that woman, that her sisters saw she was that woman. Nicole was worried that if a man touched her she would respond in a negative way. Eventually, ejaculation would be the end, yet the beginning was listening, falling subordinate to their every move.

Watching her "sister" crawl around the room on her knees gave her motivation to be better than she thought she was. Keisha was proud of her actions. Embarrassment was far from her mind. She embraced the attention and the lesson he offered. Just as he called attention to their actions, the room fell silent. The music hummed over the speakers, and his voice was clear. She was his bitch for the night, and they all knew it. Nicole was slightly jealous. He was a man of strength; curious, so she lay next to them. A man lay with her, and that was when she experienced her first touch. Keisha was upside down, and Nicole was looking in her eyes. It was sinful how her moans caused Nicole to react in such a demeanor. The wetness from her womanhood was warm and straddling her fingers. She was unsure of her next step, but she remembered touching Keisha's breast, she remembered rubbing her legs and enjoyed the attention that came along with it. Her hair hung down and swung back and forward. He continued to find her nectar sweetness.

    She found her sweet nectar; the man that lay next to her kissed her thighs. The beginning always started with passion and the end always was ejaculation at any feasible, unladylike effect. She thrust her hand inside of herself and wrapped her mouth around the head of his penis. She had carried out this operation many times in her life; however, she was looking forward to this interaction. She wanted him in her body in some form. It was informal because she didn't know his name, she didn't speak a word to him, but he had the courage to ravish her. He was soon overstimulated to the point of ejaculation. Nicole, on the other hand, was nowhere near ready but she faked it. He was a white male who must have dreamed of being with an African Queen, and that was what she gave him, his dream come true.

    After the show was over, everyone mingled back to their private corners, and indulged in more sexual activity. It was truly a sight to see. The Jojoba sister who put the grand finale show on was in the wash room when she noticed that Jojoba herself was talking to the extravagant male who was a part of the show. He talked to her as if he had known her for a while He brushed her hair off her shoulders, went into his double-breasted suit jacket that he held at his side and handed her an envelope. The way she opened it made Nicole believe it was money. Fingering through the bills, she folded the envelope and walked away. Nicole's eyes followed her to the restroom; she was so focused on Jojoba that she paid no attention to the elite gentleman that was trying to talk to her. Once the restroom door closed behind her, she had no choice but to turn to him. As he reached for her, she initially jumped. It was as if she forgot where she was and that scared her. Nicole's past was supposed to be that, her past. And here it was, knocking on her current life. She took control of the situation before it went bad. Nicole kissed him, made the first move, and made him believe he was in control. She stuck her tongue in his mouth; she wanted to be better than his obedient bitch. She wanted him to cherish her. Nicole was willing to crawl on the floor for him and she was going to show him. Instead, he pushed her off of him; he rejected her. She didn't understand why, but he did. With stiffness in his eyes, he apologized and said she had him confused. Woozy from alcohol and rejection, Nicole sat back and said, "What then, if not sex what do you want from me?" She soaked in her misery. But she licked her wounds and walked away. He grabbed Nicole's arm and stopped her. His eyes had a concerned look in them. Unsure of what to do next, she listened. His words were brilliant. He said, "She had to be his woman." He was willing to pay her to be a watchwoman over Keisha. She thought to herself she must have some good pussy. She knew she could get laid at the parties, but to get paid for babysitting was even better. Each party, she could earn fifteen hundred dollars. After a few parties, that would pay for her to find a decent apartment and a piece of a car. There was one more day of partying left, and she would be left to get settled in into her new life. She savored on the idea of providing for her daughter with a better life. Nicole became his eyes, and he became her piggy bank.

    The first down payment was three thousand dollars. Nicole wanted to ask why he walked around with so much money, but she kept her mouth closed and pocketed her money. The bell rang for their ten-minute warning that the party was coming to an end. The bathroom door opened while he talked to her; first, it was Jojoba and then minutes later, the twins. Holding her hand, he whispered in her ear and said, "No one is to know." She felt a sense of betrayal but what was she to do? She had to live and her daughter had to eat. What harm could be done with being his eyes? Nicole could have chosen to be naïve but she had no choice. She could have walked away, but she didn't.

He was a retired Marine who had been married for a short time. His wife decided to divorce him because she was tired of being alone when he was out on tour. She wanted children, and he refused. This was the information that he gave up, and the rest Nicole waited until he volunteered it. The more time she spent with him, the more she found herself in love with this man. Fluent didn't deserve him or his kindness. There was nothing she could do to gain his undivided attention. At times, it pissed her off because Keisha paid him little to no mind. Everything he did for her was to make her fall in love with him. Nicole felt as if she was the ugly stepchild that no one wanted. She hated that feeling. He continued to reject her, yet she was persistent. She became thirsty for the love he offered Keisha, and the best she could get was money and maybe sucking his dick. He treated her like his whore after a few more weeks, grabbing her, telling instead of asking, rushing instead of being patient. He became the asshole of a man that she knew all men could be.

The Investigation

They were all there telling their story because they felt they had nothing to hide. They volunteered to be questioned. They were cooperating with the investigation. Nicole's daughter has been with the babysitter for hours, they have not allowed her to make any calls, they refused to tell her if she was under arrest, and she was restless. She was thirsty and cold. *"At what point and time, will you be honest with yourself? They have nothing on any of them. They loved all of their sisters. None of them killed her*.

Nicole said, "She killed herself with her cockiness. She thought she was better than us. She knew that the men loved her but wanted to make her sisters jealous or something. I am not sure why she did the things she did but she did them. She was going to get kicked out because I became honest with Jojoba. She would meet the men outside of the meetings, taking money from them, loving them on her own time. She was not supposed to do that."

"The support group that we have is supposed to be a sisterhood. She made it about herself. Her own greed is what leads to the day of destruction for us. I got the call at my apartment at four o'clock in the morning. Jojoba asked me to fly to Nevada. I wanted to question her, but the urgency in her voice made it clear that I needed to get there. Using frequent-fliers' miles, I was there in less than twelve hours. The crime scene had been cleaned up but the blood was there. Her blood crawled up the walls. The yellow tape said in big black letters "CRIME SCENE." I was in shock! In the absence of my voice, tears filled my senses. I didn't understand why, what was happening. This was not supposed to be. She has not died, and I was not willing to accept it. Each of my sisters stood strong around the tree outside of her home. The sirens were lingering behind us. The noise of the neighbors was fading, and we were left to hold one another. We wanted justice. We called in favors. Made phone calls and persisted the truth be told. We came to you for the truth, and now you judge us for our joy and pleasure for sex. Who did this, beat her, and broke her nose in two different places? They did not want her beauty to be seen anymore. They cut her hair and spread it about in her home. And when they finished, they placed her in a bathtub of water, they had candles throughout the house. I believe this was a crime of passion."

Chapter 24
Detective Phil

"A crime of passion you say? Let me explain what a crime of passion is in simple form to you. A crime of passion is a crime committed under the influence of sudden or extreme passion. It reduces a murder charge to a manslaughter charge, and hence, reduces a defendant's possible punishment! Crime of passion results in assault or murder; it happens with jealous rage or heartbreak. Who do you believe would love her so much and hate her beauty so much that they would want to take it away from her and themselves? Did she have any boyfriends that may not approve of her belonging to Jojoba Essence? Nicole, you sitting there in silence is not cooperating. You say you all love her and that you want to help the investigation, but currently you are hindering the process of catching who did this horrible crime. The home of your friend was filled with hate not love. Someone was jealous of her or her actions."

"I'll have you to know that I am sitting here, thinking just how long it will be before I get to leave here."

"It will take as long as it needs to until you decide to tell me the truth. Your friend has died a tragic death, and the best you can tell me is she had male friends through your agency of sexual pleasures? Do you understand that your sisterhood group is all being interviewed, and as it stands, they believe you were the one with the jealous problem? The lights of her apartment were tampered with. Someone cut the main line to her electricity. This forced her to enter a dark home, possibly stumbling over the objects placed in front of her door. Thus, her bags would have not been spread across the floor. The chair in front of the door does not belong there, and I can't think of a reason why she would need it there, unless she was trying to keep someone out of her apartment."

"What are you trying to explain to me? You believe that I had something to do with this?"

"Well, yes; you were mad because the man who loved her treated you like you were less than her, even though you gave him so much attention. You threw your love at him, and he did not care or love you the same as you loved him. He loved how she sucked and obeyed him."

"Is that so?"

"Yes."

"The lack of love is what got me here. Maybe you didn't hear my story that I told you before. I was a child of prostitution; human trafficking as they call it in Minnesota. The lack of love is the reason why I am here, telling you the truth. The lack of love is more than a man holding me, or smiling in my face. Lack of love is being fifteen and having a man the age of a father, beat me because I jumped when he wanted to nut in my face. The lack of love is what my daughter's father gave me when he wanted to take her from me. See, what you think is the lack of love is nothing more than my power to survive. There have been many men that I chose to love and many more that I chose to ignore. So that lack of love is nothing that I am concerned with. One thing a black woman knows how to do is make it on less.

My black on black leather, extended 2010 Yukon truck loves me every time I gas her up and drive down whatever boulevard it wants to turn down. I started off in the streets of Minneapolis, and the alleys in garbage dumpsters of Duluth, MN. Miami Convention Center was the beginning to the woman I am, and from there, I went across the bridge and got my first apartment for seven hundred and fifty-two dollars; two bedroom one bath, small living room and even a smaller kitchen. You have to understand; today, I live in a gated community, ring my buzzer to get in. But don't let me not want to see you, through my cameras I can chose to ignore you. I laugh at those who chose to take a chance of depending on my generosity.

And now, I am laughing at you, because for some reason, you would think I would kill her over love that I have never experienced. The bright lights and lack of fresh air is temporary. My home and my daughter is nearly a blink away. Now, if you are finished with me, I would like to go."

"Actually I'm not done, but here is something to think about. If the lack of love is truly why you got here, can those very same material things that you bought with the money, watching and telling the details of her life to a man who treated you like garbage, love you back?"

"Maybe not, but my daughter will not have to worry about the lack of anything as long as money is to be made. Her hugs are priceless; the way she looks at me and kisses me goodnight is more than I could wish for. So, the lack of love you keep trying to throw in my face is nothing more than a negative thought that you may keep to yourself."

He told her, "You may leave, but don't leave the area because I will have more questions for you."

"In two weeks, my daughter and I are going to Scotland. You can call my lawyer."

Watching her walk away, he can see why men would get lost in the woman she became. The extra switch in her hips called men to her. Shaking her off, he turned to find another woman passing by him. They met at the end of the hall and hugged one another. Another sister! The hall began to fill with sexy, seductive women. He called truth to their journey of essences a sexual healing. Curious, he watched until the last of them slithered out the door. The devil wears Prada, Coach, Michael Kors, and Silver Jeans, along with the two-inch Jessica Simpson heels with the matching oversized purse and jacket. These women were dangerous.

What a mess.

Chapter 25
Chief of Police

Pissed, Phil walked into the precinct, shaking his head. There was not one lead to the murder of this young woman.

They protected one another as if they were in the Bayou's beauty, pink and purple flowers hiding among the trees. Their secrets lay beneath the surface of such activeness; it was as high as the sky and as deep as the sea. These women's secrets were well hidden. The trust among them had to be broken. They are ridiculous to think that they would get away with hiding a murderer. Tracking these women was a chore. Each had more than a small amount of money to share between them all. There was a time women knitted their shirts and blankets. The case is a mess. Something needed to be done about it.

"Transferred!"

"Sorry, there was nothing I could do; I got the order before you walked in."

"Did they say why?"

"No, it's an upper call, and the answers that you are looking for are obsolete."

"Which means what?"

"There is no need to ask them."

"Here is your file."

"Narcotics?"

"What am I going to do in narcotics? I work homicide."

"You are going to learn your new position and it starts now; pack your stuff and go to the eighth floor."

"I have no say-so, no answers, I have to just do. Then what happens to the case? Who is taking it over?"

"The fact is the murder case is going to be investigated, but hauling those women in here is what got you transferred. It's apparent they have connection in high and low places. Then what? They were the best lead we had for the death of this young woman. She was a part of a dangerous sex-filled support group. Diamonds and pearls can make anyone do wrong. Did you see her sister? She was in a daze and shock, and they lived there together. How do we know that she was not supposed to be killed but her sister ended up dead?"

"We shouldn't overlook the obvious, right? You don't have to worry about that now; you are no longer on the case. Pass the information on to Detective Christopher."

"Chief, he's new. My experience alone is older than him."

"Give him the file, your ideas, and go to the eighth floor; this is no longer up for discussion, dismissed."

"And close my door!"

Detective Christopher

Morning coffee at this place seems to get worse, and the donuts are hard.

"Eventually, I am going to go crazy if I don't get out of here." The heat is steaming up the windows and the AC is not working.

Slapping papers on his desk; Detective Phil said, "Here's the murder on 180th Street. Young dead beauty was found in her bathtub without her face and a twisted motive."

"We're partners?"

"No, it's yours. Go over it with tooth and nail. There is a serious crime here and someone has to be punished for it. Start with Jojoba Essence."

He began reading case H9B5789-00; she was a beautiful creature. The company she kept was gorgeous. Her sister found her less than an hour of her being dead. She was floating in her own blood and warm water. Parts of her flesh were found plastered on the wall panel. Her sister's memory of her will forever be distorted. Teshia saw Keisha's hands were tied together with some kind of cloth. Her hands were clenched tight with only a small amount of silk fibers under her nails. It was unknown if the perpetrator was a male or female. There was a rubber band found in her bedroom closet with black lettering wrote into it, "He hurt me." The detective couldn't make sense of it. Did it have anything to do with the case? Was it her writing or was it a ploy to detour the police from the truth? Water stains were found on the carpet. Assuming the water came from the individual who put her in the bathtub, they wanted to cleanse her. Were they thinking her spirit was dirty for her actions? They removed the skin off her face with a sharpened blade, maybe even a razor. It was a clean cut! Whoever did this violated her in every aspect of her life. Glancing over the photos of her body and of her home sent chills over Detective Chris's body. They eradicated her body but the cause of death was strangulation. Fingertip to fingertip, he prayed the heat of hell knocking would knock on the souls of those who committed this crime. The wall-mounted phone's cord was wrapped around her neck. This work of a madman was exquisite. This was a cold-blooded murder!

Since the case was at a dead-end, he needed to get away and come back with fresh eyes. Going for a mini-vacation Chicago was going to be the only way he could relax. It had been years since the last time he visited his friend. Working months on this case and he was exhausted. Twelve-hour days and nothing to show for it! No force of entry! Nothing was missing. The chief was knee-deep in his ass every week looking for more information. There was nothing to give. He looked over the paperwork until he was blue in the face. There were no fingerprints except of those who resided in the home. The fibers of the silk material belonged to her. They came from her scarf that she wore that day, but the scarf was missing. No blood whatsoever from the other victim. It was if she killed herself. The trail of evidence led him nowhere. He felt like a fucking failure! The mother and adopted parents were on the phone with him so much, he had to finally ask them for time to do his job. The bottom line was, he was at a lost.

Chapter 26
What a Vacation

Tip always tried to get him to visit Chicago, Illinois. Why not? He had the vacation hours, and his chief wanted me to step away. The community members of Chicago were either rich or poor. The middle class had become the working poor. There was no happy medium. It was one extreme to the next! Tip was drafted as a baseball star for the New York Yankees and had retired in Chicago to be near his daughter. He had nothing but money and time on his hands. He owned a condo in downtown Chi Town, as he calls it.

He hopped on the second train. Detective Christopher arrived early in the morning. He wasn't impressed with the city his good friend loved so much. Christopher became hot and sweaty while waiting on Tip's driver. The heat choked the moisture out of his throat and skin. He felt like he caught the train in the ground level of destruction. The men were selling drugs, babies were crying and young females dressed too slummy. The elder's body language suggested they were full of fear or disguise. Tip laughed when Chris said he was taking the train.

"Man, you never got over your fear of heights?"

"Hell naw."

His mind couldn't stay away from work very long. There was a motive for murder, and he was going to find it; however, he had to get it off his mind, or his whole trip would be ruined. There was nothing like a hot shower to clear a person's mind. Tip's maid handed him warm sixteen-hundred-count bath towels. It amazed him what money could introduce a person to. After his shower, he stood in the middle of the room on the left wing of his condo. Speaking over the intercom, he instructed him to look in the closest and dress in the Kenneth Cole button-down. The cufflinks were on the dresser and Christopher's initials were on them. He went all out. Hell it wasn't even his birthday. He was out of his element. Tip dealt with high-class people, and he didn't want Chris to embarrass himself. Chris figured this was about not embarrassing him. Six hours later, they arrived at the Hilton's exclusive ballroom. The Hilton was nowhere in sight; the logo was, but no hotel. Chris couldn't shake a feeling of uneasiness. But he went along with the flow. Tip instructed his driver to wait for him. Cars came, but none were allowed to leave. They were paid hefty salaries to sit in a dark parking lot.

Tip looked Chris in the eyes and said, "Real names are never used."

Chris asked, "What the hell is my name?"

"Let me make this clear. What you see hear has to stay here."

"Your name is Black."

"Black?"

"Why Black? I'm German and Italian."

"That's why, because you are not African American."

"Believe me, this is the way to go. You will never see these women again, and if you do, you will have a new name."

The ladies only knew him as Tip.

"Are we at a whorehouse?"

"What's wrong with you, dude? Whores wouldn't know what to do with me. Everything is legal."

Eventually Tip told his friend to relax and enjoy the evening. Walking into the gallery, the walls were filled with art that Chris couldn't put a name to. The aroma that came from the kitchen that was unexplainable. The women were gorgeous. They were real; when he said I could pick any type of woman, he was not far from the truth; there were different shapes, sizes, and colors. Dressed alike, they all maintained their own identity. Each had a black rose in their hair. When he entered the room, he saw the banner *"JOJOBA ESSENCE."* He was in a walking nightmare.

"How could you not tell me where the hell we were going?" He was frozen in place.

Tip tapped him on the shoulder with the biggest grin on his face. "Will you be able to relax here?"

His breath was lost somewhere between his lungs and throat. Chris couldn't speak, not even when Tip introduced him to Jojoba, otherwise known as Salina herself. He had never seen her in person. Chris only had the pleasure of speaking with her over the phone. Chris disguised his voice and his paranoid feeling. While speaking with Jojoba, a waitress walked the room collecting cell phones. No one was allowed to have a phone except Jojoba. Chris wanted to call his chief, but had no lines of communication. Chief was either going to kill him or be proud of him. He was sitting in front of food and couldn't focus on it.

The spread was immaculate: crab, lobster, shrimp, shell steak, and cheeses. Fruit bowls were full of a variety of berries; he couldn't name them all, blueberries, raspberries, kiwis, and more. The enlightenment of Jojoba Essence was these women were not sex-crazed. They were classy, intelligent, bright women. Tip knew these women like the back of his hands. They made a toast to a fallen sister, bowed their heads and kissed the rim of their glasses. This enterprise was full of surprises. The waiters and host removed the dishes, and the lights dimmed.

The music played softly in the background. It was meant to interrupt the conversation. Teddy Pendergrass, "Come Go with Me" played. Tapping his feet, Chris let his mind absorb the words Teddy Pendergrass said. He needed to move around. Wandering, Chris found himself in front of the bar. Scotch on three rocks, no chaser. His mind began racing. *If I don't participate, I will look like a damn fool and possibly a suspect.* He wandered some more.

A young lady walked up to Chris and he was staring at his victim. The lady he was trying to find justice for. She stood in front of him, her breasts set up on her chest as if no one had ever touched them.

Reaching out, he rubbed the outer surface of her face. He traced where his victim had been cut. Her face had been replaced. She was a beauty no one person should endure alone. She didn't move. She kissed the palm of his hand, and without hesitation he jerked his hand away. Looking away, she felt rejected. Teshia started to walk away; within an instant, he stopped her. He didn't want her to leave. Taking her right hand, he spun her in a circle to see exactly what she had to offer. Turning slow, he noticed she had a beauty mark on her left shoulder not her right. This was her twin. The black rose fell out of her hair. Ignoring it, they walked. The feeling of nausea settled in his stomach, and it wasn't going anywhere. They returned to the table and finally introduced themselves.

"My name is Black."

"My name is Double Knot."

She carried this sadness that he could see in her eyes. When she said her name, she looked like she was going to cry. He asked if everything was okay. She said, "Not really; this evening is in honor of my sister's death. I have lost her to a tragedy that I can't shake." He expressed how sorry he was to hear that. He felt like he was taking advantage of the situation. This could be the break that he needed; maybe she knew something that her parents and lawyer wouldn't allow her to say to him. She was ready to lie down and open her body to him. Then, they were interrupted by a toast from Tip. When Tip began speaking, Black watched her sadness. He saw her shift in her seat and became uneasy with each word spoken. She was gifted in hiding how she was feeling from others, but he has seen it so much in his career, that he couldn't help but allow his professional skills to show through. He offered her a shoulder and one of many sisters rescued her from his grasp. Slipping into the back, she returned with merely a black lace thong. Her breasts appeared soft and ready for the tasting; she appeared to me unsure of herself than she did before with clothes on. The toast was still going, but woman after woman went into the back and removed their clothing. Each with a different color lace thong on! I felt like I was in an erotica cult.

Black was amazed that they spoke of such sisterhood and her body wasn't warm in the ground for a year before they were at it again. They didn't hesitate to indulge in sex and lots of it. These women are bad girls in every sense of the statement. He learned Tip paid a hefty ten thousand dollar down payment for him. At the end of the evening, five thousand would be returned. This was a black-and-white event. All of the women were dressed like Marilyn Monroe earlier. Blonde wigs and white dresses in different forms, tight fitting, long and flowing. Now they were naked, and his dick was harder than times thirty-nine. Watching them mingle, it was a chore to keep his hands to himself. Tip appeared from behind the wall. Walking straight towards Black, his face read something different from the jolly fella he came here with. Everything was uniform; the men wore the Kenneth Cole clothing line.

Black figured her killer is here. It could be any of the men that were here, or any of her pretend sisters. Maybe she knew something the rest of the other women didn't know, and Jojoba herself got rid of her. Either way he was going to find out, and tonight was the night to do just that, especially since they were all right here.

When Tip reached him, Black asked, "Is it the same men and women that come here?"

Lost in thought, he turned around and snapped, "What did you ask me?"

Black was taken aback at his change in behavior. Realizing what had just happened, he apologized. "I just had a disturbing conversation with one of the ladies. The young lady you were speaking with is a twin, and apparently her twin was killed in Nevada in their home."

"Did you know her?"

"Yes, I mean no."

"Which one is it?"

"Both. I knew her from here but not from the real world."

The real world, he thought.

There is a difference, for sure. "She was my best bitch. I had never experienced public lovemaking before her. Our first time was unbelievable."

"Sounds like you did more than fuck her, Tip."

"Tip responded I loved her! There was nothing I could do about it. I hated to see her with other men. She made it clear she did not come here for a husband. She was strong and independent."

His friend said, "Sounds like it."

Tip asked, "You want to get out of here?"

"Thanks but no. I want to have a good time. Leaving will not bring her back; besides you still need to relax."

"Oh yeah, relaxing!"

"The young lady that I have been talking to, I think I will have her relax me."

"Good choice, but she's picky. If you get her to do it, enjoy every bit of her. I tried to get her and her sister together and that didn't go well at all. Her name fits her, she's flexible. I have watched her many times."

"We have to fuck with everyone watching?"

"You don't have to, but just know that just because you don't want to, doesn't mean you will not see it. Hilton has private rooms for people to enjoy themselves."

Leaving him where he stood, Black approached her this time, placing his hand on her hip. She flinched, and he straddled her. He asked her if she wanted to go to a private area. To his surprise, she said, "Yes." Leading him to the back, they arrived at a room that was completely dark. She took her key out from the pocket of her thong. He'd never seen that before! He accepted it and followed her in. Leaving the light off, she cased this room before entering. She led him to the bed and turned on the lamp next to the bed. He couldn't have anticipated what was going to happen next, if someone told him it was going to happen.

Chapter 27
Teshia

She was her better half-sister. When her memory came to her sister, she felt every tragic moment of it. Teshia explained they were out shopping, and she returned home before her because she had a date with her high school sweetheart. Keshia wanted out. She was in love before they got involved in this, but she pushed her sister. When they walked away from this "support group," everything would be in place for them. Because she listened to her, she is now dead. There is no preparation for the death of a sibling. Her sister died with a part of her still connected.

As she talked to him, tears streamed down her face Teshia slipped out of his grip. Never wiping the tears from her face, she allowed them to land on her breasts. Her voice lowered to a quick whisper. Listening for the others, they sat in silence. Moments passed, and she resumed with her thoughts. They created a galaxy of a world within Jojoba Essence. Tip knew about her actions through another sister in the group. She didn't know who she was, but somehow he knew her every move.

Her sister was a bigger part of her. They planned out their entire life. "Now that she is gone, who do I have? No one!" She was completely undressed, and she finally noticed the French horn playing on the surround sound speakers mounted on the wall.

"I said too much." One time, a guy named King walked up to both her and her sister. She remembered it happened six months prior to her death. He told them they were going to die soon. Maybe he'd hired a contractor! They thought he was crazy and walked away. He was slow-moving and focused so much on his shoes that he never looked up at them. Now that her sister was dead, she felt like King went to their home to kill them. The last thing she said to her sister was, "Thanks, sis, I really needed this."

Next thing she knew, she went home and the door was open. She was nervous as she went into the house, but she figured she ran to the restroom to go pee. Keisha hated the public restrooms in the mall. She would wait, go home and knock down the door so she could go in her own room in the nude. She wasn't sure why she was telling him everything.

Chapter 28
Jojoba

Something is different about all of these guys. Tip is walking around there like he has a chip on his shoulder; he brought a new guy and didn't tell anyone. She requested his attention in the kitchen. She wouldn't tell anyone that jealously became a large part of her life. Jojoba was mad that Keisha had the ability to have Tip where she wanted him. Jojoba didn't feel sorry about her death. Paying King the fifteen thousand dollars over her simple-ass life was easy.

Just as she was finishing up her thought, he turned his sexy ass around the corner with that dark chocolate skin and those soft brown lips. Looking him straight in his eye, she reached out and tried to wrap her arms around him. He moved back away from her, which made her stumble. He caught her, but that upset Jojoba. Raising her hand to slap the shit out of him, he pushed her to the floor.

"I don't hit women, but I will slap the hell out a bitch. I'm tired of you. I have tried several, if not hundreds of times, to give you respectable hints. I am not interested in you. You know who I love. Now she is dead, and you are back trying to fuck me. Tell me why you summoned me back here in this hot-ass kitchen."

"Tip, we started off better than this. It was me who introduced you to the game. I helped you make hundreds of thousands of dollars. So, you also made sure your piece of the pie was sufficient. Those who earned the least amount of money were the ones doing all the work."

"Yeah, my baby told me how you gave her five thousand dollars the first night I met her. I knew then you were a snake. Convincing these women was another thing. You are no more than a two-faced bitch. I will not let you do her the way you did her sister. Are you done yet, because I am certain I have a friend here who came to relax?"

"Who the fuck is he? I thought we agreed if you ever brought new people with you, you would let me know ahead of time? How do I know if he's FEDS or not?"

"Duh, bitch, because if he was, he would have blown the spot up. Give me a break. I have better things to do than worry about the pennies you make through this shit."

"Tip...Tip...Tip...Tip, don't walk away from me. Damn it! Don't walk away from me!"

Chapter 29
Black

"If I tell you who I am, will you yell?"

"Are you the man who killed my sister?"

"No, on the contrary; I am the man who is working to finding her killer."

"You are here undercover and trying to fuck me?"

"No. The fact of the matter is, my guy Tip brought me here."

"Tip is your fucking friend?"

"Yes, he is. What's wrong with that?"

Double Knot became terrified. She pulled out her cell phone and a 9-mm. She aimed her gun at his head. Demanding that he stand up, she forced him to go into the main meeting area. As she walked him to the middle of the floor, everyone stopped everything they were doing. A female began screaming and the crowd began rushing towards the door. Tip was several feet away from his good friend.

"What the fuck is going on?"

"Put that thing down before you find yourself in a world of shit."

"No! Who the fuck did you bring in here?"

"My guy. What the fuck did I tell you?"

"Put the damn gun down."

Jojoba started screaming Double Knot's name.

Tip went to grab her and she started to pull the trigger.

"Tip, my sister told me how you were stalking her. We saw the guys sitting outside our house every day."

"Yes, and I did it for her protection. You don't understand. She was out for your sister because your sister had me. I did that for her good. And now, I am trying to protect you because I was unable to protect her."

"Who is she?"

"Jojoba!"

"Tip, you want to tell me what the hell is going on?"

Jojoba yelled, "Don't believe that shit! He killed your sister!"

Tip said, "Baby-girl listen to this; I have no reason to lie to you, I loved your sister, and she knew it. Jojoba hated your sister for it. I wouldn't be surprised if she did it. But, I want you to listen to this so you know I'm not lying," Tip explained.

"I don't hit women, but I will slap the hell out a bitch. I'm tired of you. I have tried several, if not hundreds of times, to give you respectable hints. I am not interested in you. You know who I love. Now she is dead, and you are back trying to fuck me. Tell me why you summoned me back here in this hot-ass kitchen."

"Tip, we started off better than this. It was me who introduced you to the game. I helped you make hundreds of thousands of dollars. So, you also made sure your piece of the pie was sufficient. Those who earned the least amount of money were the ones doing all the work."

"Yeah, my baby told me how you gave her five thousand dollars the first night I met her. I knew then you were a snake. Convincing these women was another thing. You are no more than a two-faced bitch. I will not let you do her the way you did her sister. Are you done yet, because I am certain I have a friend here who came to relax?"

"Who the fuck is he? I thought we agreed if you ever brought new people with you, you would let me know ahead of time? How do I know if he's FEDS or not?"

"Duh, bitch, because if he was, he would have blown the spot up. Give me a break. I have better things to do than worry about the pennies you make through this shit."

"Tip...Tip...Tip...Tip, don't walk away from me. Damn it! Don't walk away from me!"

Tip stopped the tape recorder. "I loved your sister, and I wanted to marry her; she kept turning me down because of this sisterhood."

As Double Knot listened attentively to Tip, Chris was able to wrestle the gun out of her hand.

Jojoba screamed, "Those are all lies, and I think you are stupid to believe him."

Double Knot fell to the floor from exhaustion and fear.

Tip said, "The tape speaks for itself. Jojoba, you need to hand me the phone."

"What the fuck for?"

"Because the authorities need to be notified."

The exhaustion Double Knot experienced caused her to break out in a cold sweat. She lay on the floor in a cradle position and sobbed for her loss. Jojoba tried to run to her side, but Tip grabbed her. "Leave her alone."

The doors swung open. The crowd of half-dressed women and men continued to run out of the building. The first group of couples ran to a driver and requested they call the police.

Moments passed as Jojoba continued to beg for Double Knot to listen to her. Her pleas went unheard.

"Salina Johnson, you are under arrest for the murder of Keisha Smith. You have the right to remain silent. Anything you say can and will be used against you in a court of law. You have the right to an attorney. If you cannot afford one, one will be appointed to you. Do you understand?"

Jojoba dropped to her knees.

CPSIA information can be obtained
at www.ICGtesting.com
Printed in the USA
FFOW03n2038041117
43281545-41832FF